THE BOY WHO WANTED PEACE

George Friel

UNABRIDGED

PAN BOOKS LTD : LONDON

First published 1964 by John Calder (Publishers) Ltd.
This edition published 1972 by Pan Books Ltd,
33 Tothill Street, London, S.W.1

ISBN 0 330 02913 4

Printed in Great Britain by
Richard Clay (The Chaucer Press), Ltd,
Bungay, Suffolk

THE BOY WHO
WANTED PEACE

Reviewing *The Boy Who Wanted Peace*, Anthony Burgess called it 'the work of a brilliant and original novelist'. The BBC commissioned an adaptation for radio and television and it has been shown as one of the Wednesday plays.

George Friel was born in Glasgow in 1910 and has used his intimate knowledge of the city and its people to provide the background and characters for his novels. He was educated in St Mungo's Academy and Glasgow University where he edited the University Magazine. After working as a public-house waiter, insurance collector, inquiry agent and schoolmaster, he joined the Army and served in the Ordnance Corps. His publications include *The Bank of Time, Grace and Miss Partridge,* which received an award from the Scottish Arts Council in 1969, and *Mr Alfred MA*.

THE BOY WHO
WANTED PEACE

CHAPTER ONE

Hugh O'Neill and Shaun O'Donnell, two big broad Glasgow Irishmen who claimed to be descended from Niall of the Nine Hostages who was King of All Ireland when the ancestors of the English aristocracy were grubbing for nuts in the forest, bumped into each other getting off the same bus at Parkhead Cross just as the pubs were opening. The sky was blue, the syvers were littered, and there was the clinging smell of decaying refuse that goes with a warm spring evening in the East end of the city. They were parched, hot and sticky after a hard day's work, and with a little jerk of the head and a question in their royal blue eyes they understood each other at once and went into the Tappit Hen for a brotherly crack over a quiet drink before going on home for their tea. They were only a couple of workers from the Yards who built more ships talking shop of an evening at the bar than ever they built in a year's work, but their conversation on this occasion may throw some light on the events that began the same evening, though they themselves were of course unaware of the coincidence.

'What'll ye have?' O'Donnell asked since he happened to be the first through the swing doors.

'A glass and a pint,' O'Neill answered, raising one hand high to salute the barman. The shade and coolness of the place were pleasant to him after the heat and dust outside. He liked pubs especially when they had just opened. At that time they were as dim and quiet as a church. A man could be at peace there with a drink in front of him, and the gantry was a kind of altar. Certainly it held on its glass shelves the expensive liquid that made life bearable and sometimes even enjoyable – uisgebeatha in the language of the Gael, the water of life in the language of the Saxon.

7

'A glass and a pint!' O'Donnell repeated in alarm, his Irish eyes reproachful. 'Do ye think I've been robbin' a bank? Ye'll have a half and a half-pint and like it.'

They stood in reverent silence till they were served.

'Funny you saying robbing a bank,' said O'Neill. 'I was just reading in the paper there coming in on the bus. See the Colonel's deid.'

'Oh aye, the Colonel, aye, so he's deid, is he,' said O'Donnell. Not until he had put a little water in the whiskies did he try to understand what they were talking about. He frowned. 'How do ye mean, the Colonel?'

'The Colonel I mean,' said O'Neill. 'Him they got for the Anderston bank robbery. He's deid.'

'Oh, I see, God rest his soul,' said O'Donnell with routine sorrow in his flat voice.

'The paper was saying he died in jail,' said O'Neill. 'Well, no' in the jail exactly, it was in the infirmary, but he was still in jail of course because it was eight years he got.'

'Funny,' said O'Donnell. 'That other bloke they got for the Ibrox bank robbery, he died in jail last month as well.'

'Aye, it makes ye think,' said O'Neill. 'He was a Canadian.'

'No, he was an Australian,' said O'Donnell. 'Or his pal was an Australian or wan o' them was an Australian but no' a Canadian.'

'No, he was a Canadian all right,' said O'Neill.

'No, an Australian,' said O'Donnell, finishing his whisky and elevating his beer.

'Ach, ye're thinking o' the Ibrox bank,' said O'Neill. 'That was the Major, no' the Colonel. The monocled Major they called him. He was an Australian but it was his pal that died no' him. But the Colonel was a Canadian so he was, it was the Major was an Australian.'

'That's what I'm saying,' O'Donnell complained. 'He was an Australian, him or his mate. Wan o' them.'

'Funny how these blokes come to Glasgow,' said O'Neill. He shook the dregs of his whisky glass into his beer.

'Ach, there's a lot o' folks come to Glasgow for the

8

country roon aboot,' said O'Donnell. 'They've heard o' the bonnie, bonnie banks o' Loch Lomond.'

'It's no' the banks o' Loch Lomond they fellows came for,' O'Neill retorted, pouting over the half-pint he was raising to his lips. He sipped and went on. 'It's the Royal Bank and the Clydesdale Bank and the Commercial Bank and the Bank of Scotland and the British Linen Bank, that's what they came for. Ye know, there's been a wheen o' bank robberies in Glasgow in the last five or six year. Just you think back.'

'Ach, I don't know,' said O'Donnell. 'See the Bhoys is doing well the now. Were you there on Saturday?'

'Aye I was there,' said O'Neill. 'But they're no' that clever. The polis aye catch up on them sooner or later so they do. The trouble with the Bhoys is they never keep it up. They go away and let the Thistle or the Thirds beat them when ye least expect it.'

'I don't mind so long as they beat the Rangers,' O'Donnell replied nonchalantly, offering his mate a cigarette. 'Here! But the polis are no' that clever either. They get them but they don't get the money.'

'Ye're right there,' said O'Neill. 'It says in the paper there's thirty thousand pound still missing. But the Bhoys has got youth on their side, that's mair nor the Rangers have. You can see it in the paper there for yourself.'

O'Donnell looked at O'Neill's paper.

'Funny,' he said. 'It was just the same wi' the Ibrox robbery. Forty thousand it was they didn't get. But I'd never take the Bhoys in my coupon.'

'Oh naw, neither would I,' said O'Neill. 'And then there's Napper Kennedy. Maryhill. They got him in Dublin but they never got the money. Oh naw, I'd never take them in the pools. Ye canna trust them.'

'They got some of it did they no'?' said O'Donnell. 'Somebody left a suitcase in the left luggage. It was his brother wasn't it in the Central Station?'

'Aye, they got five thousand,' said O'Neill. 'Nothing much. There was mair nor thirty thousand they never got yet. And there's Charlie Hope, him that done the Partick bank. He never got as far as Dublin. They got him in his club in St Vincent Street. A bridge club he called it, some bridge club. But they got damn all else but the smell o' his cigar. That was another thirty or forty thousand job. They boys have something to come out to so they have.'

'Ach, they'll never get near it,' said O'Donnell. 'What I say is, the Bhoys ought to spend money on a good inside forward. They've got a lot o' good young yins but the young yins need an auld heid. They'll no' even get gaun to the lavatory without somebody on their tail.'

'Ach, I don't know about that,' O'Neill shrugged. 'They've got ways and means I'll bet you. They don't go to all that trouble for nothing. Where would ye get a good inside forward anyway? They've spent good money before this and it's been money wasted. They're better sticking tae what they've got.'

'Trouble, aye it's trouble all right,' said O'Donnell. 'Eight or nine years they get, every time. But you're right enough I suppose, some of their best servants was players they got for nothing.'

'Well, so what?' O'Neill asked. 'Would you no' do eight or nine year to come out tae thirty or forty thousand?'

'Aye, if I was coming out tae it,' said O'Donnell. 'But that's what I'm arguing, they'll no' come out tae it. The minute they touch it they'll be lifted.'

'But they've served their time, haven't they?' said O'Neill. 'They canny put them in jail twice for the wan offence.'

'That's murder you're thinking of,' said O'Donnell. 'Robbery's different. Sure they'd take the money from them, wouldn't they? They'd never let them get away wi' it. That would make it too easy. I'd do it myself for eight or nine year.'

'But suppose somebody else has been keeping it to feed it back to them when they come out, ye know, in regular payments, quiet like.'

'Who could they trust to keep thirty or forty thousand for them?' O'Donnell asked derisively. 'Would you trust anybody wi' that amount o' money if you were inside for eight or nine year?'

'I don't know,' said O'Neill thoughtfully. 'I've never had that amount o' money. Maybe ye could if ye made it worth their while. What'll ye have?'

'Just as a matter of interest, how many is that now?' O'Donnell asked.

'It's only yer second,' said O'Neill. 'You put the first wan up when we came in and that's all we've had. Do ye want the same again?'

'Naw, no' the drinks, the bank robberies I mean ye're talking about,' said O'Donnell. 'Anderston, Ibrox, Maryhill, Whiteinch, that's four at least.'

'Oh, there's been a lot mair nor that,' said O'Neill. 'And tae think it's a' lying somewhere! They're a' inside and the money's outside. Thirty thousand here and forty thousand there and the same again and the same again and mair. It would break yer heart just thinking about it.'

'Aye, it would be a bit of all right finding even wan o' they stacks. Will ye be up seeing the Bhoys on Saturday?'

'Aye, ye could find it but would ye have the nerve tae spend it?' said O'Neill. 'Och aye, I'll be there all right.'

'I'll see ye here at two o'clock then,' said O'Donnell. 'I like seeing the Bhoys when they're doing well.'

'But I'll see ye before then,' said O'Neill. 'Ye'll be in here the night aboot eight, will ye no'?'

'Och aye, sure,' said O'Donnell. 'The Bhoys is drawing big money the now all right.'

'Forty-five thousand there last Saturday,' said O'Neill.

They took no more after O'Neill had returned O'Donnell's hospitality. They were two steady working-men, and they went straight home for their tea after their second drink. They knew they would be back in the same pub in a couple of hours. And besides Glasgow's plague of bank robberies there was the state of the Yards on the Clyde to discuss, and there was the Celtic football team to talk about. For two Glasgow Irishmen that was a topic as inexhaustible as the weather to two Englishmen.

CHAPTER TWO

That same evening, in the Bute Hall, the Glasgow University Choral Society and the University Orchestra gave a performance of Bach's B Minor Mass. It was damned with faint praise by the music critic of the local paper, a sour Scotsman who complained of the acoustics and found the choir's hundred and eight voices too light for the place and purpose. O'Neill and O'Donnell, like most people in the city, didn't know the Mass was being sung by the University Choral Society, so they weren't present. They were back in the Tappit Hen before the Sanctus. But among those who did attend the Bute Hall was the unwitting hero of this true narrative, a culture-hungry teenager who had failed in his eleven-plus examination and come to life at sixteen, just after he left school. He was working as a packer in the Scottish Cooperative Wholesale Society in Nelson Street, but he knew he deserved something a lot better. He went about his daily chores with a dagger of bitterness against a system that had refused him a higher education just because he didn't happen to pass an examination when he was only twelve. He tried to educate himself. He went to the public library every night and brought home books on philosophy, psychology, economics, and the history of art from the cave-paintings to Picasso. He found his pleasure in the very act of borrowing them. When the girl stamped the date-label and filed the title-slips with his tickets he was sure she admired and respected him. Nobody else in his unjust position would have had the courage and intelligence to borrow such books. He had always to take them back before he had time to read them, but he felt that even having them in the house was something. To see Kant's *Critique of Pure Reason* on the kitchen dresser alongside the first volume of Marx's *Capital* was a great consolation to him. You never knew who might come in and see them. It only annoyed his mother. She had no patience with him.

'It's high time you took them books back,' she scolded him every time she dusted the dresser where she displayed her grandmother's two brass candlesticks, the four large seashells she had brought home from her holiday at Millport the year she was married, a photo of her mother in a white-metal frame, a snap of her brother when he was a sergeant with the Argyll and Sutherland Highlanders in Singapore, an enamelled tray showing two pastoral lovers beside a rustic bridge, and her bottle of cough mixture. 'How can I keep this corner tidy if you clutter it up with books? And they're all overdue and I never see you open them anyway.'

'You don't see all I do,' he answered, looking down on her from a great height.

'There's sevenpence to pay on each of them,' she complained the night he was getting ready to go to the Bute Hall. 'You might as well buy the damn things, the money you spend in fines. Do you think I've nothing to do with my money but give it to you to pay for all the books you keep past their time?'

'Money, money, money! All you can think of is money!'

He was peevish with her. She was always nagging him since his father died a month ago.

'Somebody's got to think about it,' she said, her head high, acting the calm lady to his bad temper. 'Of course, you're Lord Muck of Glabber Castle, you're too high and mighty to bother about money. I'd have thought now your poor father's dead at least you'd try and help your mother. You've only one mother in this world, you know, my boy.'

She wiped her eyes with a dirty hankie, and went ruthlessly on.

'Your poor father's no' here any longer to look after us now, ye know. Him dying the way he did. Puffed out like a candle. Wan minute he was there, the next he wasna. It's something I'll never get over. The day after his brother was killed. No' that he was any good. But your poor father was a good man. Do anything for anybody. Worked hard all his days. Then just to die like that, down in the cellar all by himself. And then they tried to tell me it was his heart. Funny he never complained about his heart before. Of course him and Sammy was twins. They was born together and I suppose they had to go together. Well, near enough. Sammy was killed on the Friday and your poor father was found dead the next day, couldny ha' been more than a couple of hours after he heard about it. Makes you think. You ought to be helping me, no' annoying me the way you do.'

She sniffed wetly, and his nerves jangled at the sound of air through mucus.

'I'm helping all I can,' he said dourly. 'But I never get a bloody word of thanks for it. Don't forget it's me pays the rent for the house.'

'You're lucky to have a house at all to pay the rent for,' she snapped, her nose clear again for a minute. 'Don't forget we lost a good house rent-free when your father went and died.'

'Some house,' he gibed, surveying her as if he was estimating her height and weight. How could he, so tall and handsome, come from such a shrivelled thing as this crabbit woman with grey hair, mournful eyes, a flat chest and skinny legs with black cotton stockings? It was another injustice. He should have had a beautiful elegant mother with shapely legs and a bosom like the advert for a shaving soap, not too much and not too little, a mother who would inspire him to write the poetry he knew he could write if only he could get peace and quiet. 'A janitor's house in the school playground! That's a fine house! Living right in the middle of the slum where he worked.'

'It was a bigger and better house than this,' she shouted. 'Who could I bring here, a room and kitchen up a dirty close with a stairhead lavatory, and a single-end on each landing? You never think what a come-down it is for me to have to go out to work and be a cleaner in the very school where your father was the janitor for fifteen year, aye, and his job was jist as important as the headmaster's I can tell ye. He saw them come and he saw them go, and they'd all have been lost without him. He kept them right. And now I've got to be a cleaner there and live in a room and kitchen that looks right on to the four-apartment house I had rent-free in the playground. It just shows you how life treats you.'

'You're just after saying we're lucky to be here,' he stabbed quickly back, gloating over her cracked temper. 'Lucky that big fat drip Nancy went to Canada. Ha-Ha! That was a bit of luck all right. If ever a dame got on my nerves it was her with her very coarse veins. A real intellectual topic of conversation she had!'

'You'll please me if you speak of your Aunt Nancy with proper respect for your elders,' she said stiffly, on her dignity as a lady again. 'If your Aunt Nancy hadn't got the factor to agree to us getting her house I don't know where we could have went I'm sure. And just having to flit across the street from the school was a big saving. If we'd had to pay for all our furniture getting took somewhere across the river it would have cost us a lot of money I can tell you. But you never think of that. You've a mind above money, like.'

'You aye come back to money, don't you?' he said. 'You'd think that was all there was in this life, money, the way you talk, you've no idea of art and philosophy and – and—'

He was stuck for a moment for another subject, to let her see what a superior mind he had.

'And poetry and the drama,' he added quickly, remembering the card above the shelves in the far corner of the library. 'You've never lived. I've lived, so I have. I've read the great poets, it's more than you ever done. You, you've no idea of culture.'

'Have you?' she asked him very coolly, cutting him deep. 'You couldn't even pass your qually and you try and kid me about culture. You never read the half of the books you bring in here.'

'Ach!' he snarled at her.

'Another thing,' she pursued him cruelly, turning from the cracked, mottled sink where the window looked across

15

Bethel Street to the ancient school where her husband had worked. 'It's high time you stopped hanging about the back-court and going across there to the playground every night. If you could just see yourself! Be your age. It looks daft, a big fellow like you playing with wee boys at school.'

'I'm not playing with them,' he answered proudly. 'I'm helping them. They come to me for advice. Cause I'm older and cause I know more than they do. I'm trying to learn them. If I'd had somebody to guide me the way I guide them when I was their age I wouldn't be where I am today, so I wouldn't.'

'A crowd of scabby gangsters,' his mother muttered. 'There's no' a shop in the street safe from them.'

'Okay they've got a gang,' he admitted generously. 'And what's wrong with having a gang? A gang is only the expression of the primitive need for a community. You read any book on child-psychology, that'll tell you. People feel they must belong. I mean ordinary people. And these lads aren't even ordinary. They're a lot of poor dirty neglected children with nobody to shower love on them.'

'Shower,' his mother sniffed, having trouble with her nose again. 'They're a shower all right. Shower o' bastards.'

'Their parents have no interest in them,' he went on, making a speech at her, 'and they've no interest in their parents. They were born in the jungle and their whole existence is one fierce struggle to survive. The only law they know is the law of the jungle and they're beginning to learn its disadvantages. So they come to me and I try to learn them to live according to the law of law and order. They see you've got to have someone to appeal to so they come to me. I'm their referee. They rely on me for to see justice done. I'm the lawman. I'm the judge. Cause I stand above it so I can see it. Boys are like Jews, they're different from the people round about them. And where would the Jews have been if they hadn't had Moses to give them the Law?'

'Ach!' his mother derided him. 'Playing wi' a lot o' weans and ye call yourself Moses!'

'They're not weans,' he shouted. 'They're innocent chil-

16

dren. And Christ has said unless ye become as little children ye shall not enter the Kingdom of Heaven.'

'Oh, it's Christ now, is it?' cried his baffled mother. 'You'd gar anybody grue so you would the way you talk. Moses! Christ!'

She returned to the dishes in the basin in the sink.

At that point in their friendly discussion he banged out of the house, scampered down the three storeys to the close, went into the littered smelly street and walked across the city to the University. He liked passing through the Main Entrance in University Avenue. He felt he was entering the land he should have inherited. He often walked through the University to comfort himself. When he crossed the Arts Quadrangle and approached the Bute Hall he felt happier and lighter. All his grudges dropped from him. He was where he ought to be. If the girl in the library could see him now she would think he was a student all right. A university student, that was the life.

Bach's music didn't get over to him, but he was pleased to be sitting there while the choir and orchestra went through it. His attention drifted peacefully. Music always made his mind wander. That was why he liked to go to orchestral concerts. He felt liberated. So while the sopranos got lost in 'Cum Sancto Spiritu' he plunged contentedly through the jungle of his grievances.

All he wanted was peace, peace and quiet, and he couldn't get it. He wanted to be free from the need to earn his living so that he could be a poet like Shelley or make documentary films like Peter Scott or be a novelist like Tolstoy or even a television personality. He knew he had other talents too. He had helped to prepare and move the scenery when the Drew Rowan Youth Club put on a pantomime, and he enjoyed being back-stage. He knew he had a good sense of the theatre. He could produce plays, or he could travel round the world with a cine-camera and do a series about strange places and peculiar peoples. There was nothing hard in what David Attenborough did. Anybody could do it. All you needed was money. Anything was possible if you had the money to give you the leisure to do it. He could be an authority on modern art. Nobody else in Packing and Dispatch had read the amount of stuff he had read on Picasso and Henry Moore. Shelley and Wordsworth had enough money to write poetry without having to work as well. If they had been a janitor's son like him they wouldn't have had the chance. If he had the money he could buy a house on some lonely part of the coast in Devon or Cornwall, and it would be peaceful enough there to be a poet. To be a poet you had to see things as children saw them, all fresh and unspoilt, like the smell of apples or the colour of the sky when the sun was setting behind the Campsies in summer or the touch of a cat's fur or the taste of a glass of milk and a buttered roll. And because he liked to be with kids and listen to them blether so that he could keep roots in the world of his childhood people laughed at him. They said he was soft.

They had said he was soft since the first day he went to school. He blamed it on his name. He hated it for years. Percy was a sloppy name. It was too uncommon in the tenements, too Kelvinside, too English, to get respect. It was worst in the qualifying class, where even the teacher made jokes about it. She kept on saying he was slow in arithmetic and backward in reading and poor at spelling and hopeless at composition. Her daily crack was to tell him he must persevere.

'Ah, here's Percy again,' she said to the class every day when those with no sums right lined up for the strap. 'He tries very hard. He's very trying, is our Percy. It's a fine old English name, Percy. So is Vere.'

She raised his hand a little higher, straightened his palm, and addressed him as she strapped him.

'Well, Percy, you must Percy Vere. That's all.'

And every day the boys and girls preparing for the eleven-plus examination laughed at the same joke and laughed at him. It was the girls' laughter hurt him most. It fell from Heaven like the merriment of angels looking down on the antics of a clod-hopper who couldn't get his big feet out of the mud. He grew sullen at Miss Elginbrod's daily joke and one bright morning in May he challenged her. The room was stuffy in the early sun. Miss Elginbrod always kept the windows closed because she disliked draughts. His head was hot and he didn't know what the sums were about. It was trains one minute and marbles the next, then it was rolls of cloth, then it was tons and quarts. One minute she was saying you add the speeds, then she was saying you subtract them. She kept on hopping about. You were just beginning to think you were bringing pounds to pennies when she made you bring pounds to ounces. She never gave you peace. So for the thousandth time he had only two sums finished out of the five, both wrong, and for the thousandth time she shrugged over him.

'Well, Percy, you've just got to persevere, that's all.'

He faced her, rather round-shouldered because of his height. Even then he was much taller than other boys of his age, and it made him look gawky.

'Please, miss,' he said, and then his nerve failed.

'Yes?' said Miss Elginbrod, looking at him with patronizing patience, swinging the strap in a practice smack. 'Is there something you don't understand?'

Her question gave him back his determination to oppose her.

'I don't understand why you call me Percy Vere. My name isn't Percy Vere, it's Percy Phinn.'

An earthquake unpredicted by the eight o'clock weather forecast shook the class. A cyclone of laughter lifted the roof and a tornado of girlish screams whipped the walls apart. He felt himself naked to the wind and weather when he had expected to stand there proud and respected in an awed silence. He was frightened. There was never a mockery like this, clawing at him on all sides and tearing him apart to eat him up.

For causing a disturbance in the class Miss Elginbrod gave him three hard ones with her strap, not the thin one she always had in her hand but the thick one she kept away at the back of her desk out of sight until she was really angry. And when she had done that she said he had been insolent, and gave him another three.

When he was reborn at sixteen he looked back on his past life and blamed Miss Elginbrod for his failure in the examination. She had discouraged him. She ought to have seen he was a case of late development like Sir Winston Churchill. She ought to have seen his true merit and given him love and understanding. She wasn't fit to be a teacher. People like her would have failed to see Shelley's gifts when he was a boy at school. She had never even told him he had the same name as Shelley. She just made a joke of it. That proved she was so ignorant she didn't know Shelley's first name. He had to find it out for himself after he had left school. The discovery excited him. He stopped hating his name. He became proud of it. It made him something of a poet too. He read up on Shelley. In a biographical dictionary in the public library he found a sentence that he copied out and learned off by heart. 'Percy was a boy of much sensibility, quick imagination, generous heart, and a refined type of beauty, blue-eyed and golden-haired.' He hadn't only the same name as Shelley, he had the same colour of eyes and the same colour of hair – though his mother said his hair was 'like straw hinging oot a midden'. But his mother had no sensibility, no quick imagination. It was a mystery where his had come from. And he was a rebel too, just like Shelley. It was for being a rebel that Miss Elginbrod had given him six with her Lochgelly strap. Well, he would remember her, and when he was famous as a poet or a producer or an authority on modern art she would be ashamed of herself. But to get fame he would have to get leisure, and to get leisure he would have to get money. It always came back to money.

'If only!' he dreamed while the choir exulted in the Gloria. 'If only I had enough money to live without having to go out to work every day. If only I had a private income like Shelley and Wordsworth. I could get peace then I'd show them. If only I'd got a fair deal out of life I could play my cards better.'

CHAPTER THREE

While Percy Phinn was attending Bach's Mass a search-party was out from the gang that bowed to him as patron, chairman, and final arbiter. They were frightened, and they wanted advice. Some of them laughed at Percy behind his back, some of them argued he was 'dead clever', but they all agreed he would never do them a dirty trick and they were all scared of him a little, especially when he fixed them with his big, sad eyes and lectured them on the good life. And now they needed help from somebody clever, somebody older, somebody they could trust. It could only be Percy. That was the unanimous decision, taken in full assembly in the cellar. But they couldn't find him. He wasn't in Johnny Hay's billiards-room (billiards was the one game where he showed any talent), he wasn't in the public library, he wasn't in the house, he wasn't at the corner watching the big girls go by, he wasn't in the playground refereeing five-a-side football, he wasn't at the swings pushing the kids higher and higher, he wasn't anywhere. He had simply vanished. It showed how clever he was. They were baffled. They had never heard of the Bute Hall or Bach either. They were only ten or eleven years of age. Hughie Savage, the oldest of them, was not quite twelve. He couldn't read very well, but he was shrewd and he could write out a three-cross double with no difficulty. He was far cleverer than his teachers ever suspected, and his line of humour was to put on a la-dee-da voice and speak in what he thought was an English accent. He had a big head on a bull neck and his ears stuck out like a couple of cabbages.

The scattered groups of the search-party returned by arrangement to the cellar at half past nine. When they were all present for the second time that evening Savage took the chair and reported Percy's disappearance. The chair he sat on was a high-legged one with a broken back and a foot-rail. It was the chair Miss Elginbrod had sat on when Percy was in her class, but the back spars and the shoulder-rest came off one afternoon when she threw a cheeky boy across the room. He fell against it and knocked it over. When he got to his feet he kicked it apart in a fury while Miss Elginbrod whipped him round the legs with her strap. She sent it to the janitor for repair, and the janitor put it away in the cellar till he could find time to look at it. Death found him first, and the chair had lain there ever since, in the cellar below the school, the secret headquarters of the gang that Percy sponsored.

This was no picayune cellar. It was a sprawling low-roofed vault stretching below the main building and out under the playground, where it ended in an unexplored boundary of evil darkness. Not even Frank Garson had ever touched that far-off invisible wall, and when the Three High Clavigers of the Bethel Brotherhood ordered him to make a map of the cellar because Miss Elginbrod had praised his drawing and handwriting he left his sketch open at that side and along it he wrote in a scroll *Here Be Rats*. A door in the basement, at the end of an L-shaped line of wash-hand basins, opened to a dim and dangerous staircase that went steeply down to the bowels of the building, and that was commonly supposed to be the only door to the cellar. But because of the gradient on which the school was built there was another door to the cellar in Tulip Place, a blind alley round the corner from Bethel Street. It was a small, inconspicuous, dark-green door, hacked by many initials, and behind it was a chute. That was where the coal for the boilers had been delivered before the school changed over to electrical heating, and then the door was locked for good and forgotten.

Percy had a key to it from his father's days as janitor. Three other keys were cut from his and given to the three oldest members of the Brotherhood. The cellar became their church, the scene of enrolment, expulsion, and initiation rites. It was to be entered only from the blind alley after the school was locked up for the night. Percy found a word for the keyholders who alone had the power to permit

22

entry. He got it when he was grazing in a dictionary in the reference room of the library. He called them the Clavigers. To be a Claviger in Percy's gang was the highest rank you could reach. He gave himself the title of Regent Supreme because the boys knew those two words, but he went to great trouble to explain to them what they meant apart from their occurrence in a television advert.

Over the undated years the cellar had become a junk-house. a dark neglected dump where people threw things they didn't know what to do with. Scores of old registers, tied in tape and going back for decades, were stacked against a wall and crowned by bundles of ancient group mental tests and verbal ability tests, pupils' record cards, report cards and medical histories. Nobody had ever dared destroy them. Such documents are intimidating. They have their own over-weening life. To burn them would be as brutal and immoral as committing murder. And you could never be sure they wouldn't be wanted one day. Somebody might ask for the date of birth or the father's name or the IQ of a pupil who had left years ago and was now in Bar-linnie Prison for house-breaking. It would never do to reply, 'The records have been destroyed'. The whole point of keeping records is that they are kept after they are kept. Other-wise why keep them?

Scattered alongside these sacred but forgotten documents there were blackboard compasses, blackboard rulers, pointers, pyramids, cones, cylinders and spheres, a carton of inkwells with the bakelite rims chipped off by vandals so that they fell through the hole cut for them in the pupils' desks, the broken pole of a dead traffic warden, a punctured hose, brooms, spades, shovels and rakes, brown paper piled four feet high with the salvaged string wound round the sheets, a pail of stucco, a barrel half-full of washing-soda, empty bleach bottles put aside to be filled with ink made from a powder, political maps of Europe, Asia and Africa dating from before the first world war, a coal-scuttle and a stirrup pump. On one side of the outmoded boiler was a woodwork bench with a vice that wouldn't screw up tight, and on the other a ziggurat of broken dual desks. In front of the desks was an old piano with occasional dumb keys. It had been put there twenty-two years ago, when an insistent music-teacher asked for and got a new piano. The janitor filled in the correct form to have the old one uplifted, but somehow nothing was ever done about it. On top of the piano was the large hand-bell that had been rung to assemble and dismiss the school before the electric bells were put in. It was a heavy bell, solid brass, and Savage said it was worth at least a fiver as scrap metal, but Percy wouldn't let him hawk it.

Across the cellar from the broken desks, under a tangle of legless chairs, educational publishers' catalogues, pre-war copies of the *Scottish Educational Journal*, and five dozen derelict reading books called *The Sunshine Way*, were six tea-chests, three along and two deep, containing the costumes and small props used in the annual school concert. But there had been no annual concert for five years, and in that time there had been two new headmasters and Percy's father had died of a thrombosis, so that nobody in the school knew exactly what was in them.

There were two weak ceiling lights in the cellar, but the Brotherhood preferred not to switch them on during council meetings. They lit six candles, using the bleach bottles as candlesticks, and the dim unsteady light, with flickering shadows on the walls receding into the damp darkness where the rats were, gave a proper obscurity to the arguments of the assembly.

'I vote we carry on without the Regent,' said Hugh Savage, Chief Claviger, whose Christian name was locally pronounced 'Sheuch'.

'No, I object,' said Specky, Second Claviger, sitting on the inverted coal-scuttle to the right of Savage's chair. He was a brassy, blethering confident boy, wearing thick convex glasses with thin wire frames, a Schools Health Service issue, and he talked like a book.

'Well, we'll vote for it,' said Skinner, Third Claviger, sitting on a drawing-board placed across the pail of stucco. He was always called Skinny in affectionate abbreviation of his surname. It was only a fortuitous anomaly that he happened to be a chubby child.

The Three High Clavigers faced the ruck of the Brotherhood, obedient troopers who sat, knelt or squatted on the grimy stone floor. Savage was the strong arm, Specky was the brains and Skinny was the kind heart. In that cavernous gloom they looked like three subterranean judges addressing a jury of sooterkins.

'I'm in this,' Frank Garson shouted from the front row. 'It was me that found it. You can't decide, Sheuch. You've got to wait for Percy. That's the rule for urgent business.'

'Don't you call me Sheuch when I'm in the chair,' Savage checked him crossly. Then he leered forward. 'Anyway, how can it be urgent if we've got to wait for Percy? And you should be in the dock, so you should, but I move that Probationer Garson's expelled. Come on, get him in the dock!'

Garson was pushed and pulled by four of Savage's faction and forced to stand behind a dual desk on the left of the chair.

'What's the charge?' he screamed.

'You broke the first commandment,' said Judge Savage. 'All for one and one for all, united we stand but divided we fall. That's Percy. Percy's a poet, ye know.'

'That's our motto,' Garson objected hotly. 'It's not a commandment.'

'Doesn't matter, you still broke it,' the judge answered swiftly. 'You wanted to keep it all for yersel'. If Specky hadn't have been with you we wouldn't have knew a thing about it.'

'That's not true,' Garson shouted, wriggling in the dock between his jailers. 'Specky wouldn't have known a thing about it if I hadn't told him.'

'That's right,' Specky admitted, standing up to address the judge. 'I said it was a matter for the Brotherhood and he said we ought to tell the cops but he never said he wanted it all for himself.'

'No, of course, he wouldn't say it,' Savage complained. 'But that's what he meant to do all right. Get the bell and expel him!'

'You can't do it like that,' Specky whispered, horrified.

'That's wrong,' Skinny called out, indignant.

The campanologist, so named and appointed by Percy to perform the rituals of admission, expulsion, summoning and dispersal, grabbed the bell from the piano and Garson darted at once from the clutch of his warders and struggled with him. The bell rang irregularly as they wrestled for it.

'A barley, a barley!' Skinny yelled in distress, and the contestants stood frozen. The assembly murmured against the brawl, condemning the decision that had provoked it. Savage saw he hadn't the support for an expulsion and tried again quickly.

'I propose an equal division then. Right here and now. Elect two tellers and share it out without Percy.'

'Twenty tellers couldn't count it,' Garson protested vehemently. 'And if they could you couldn't spend it. I said the cops because I saw it was too much for us but when Specky said report it I agreed because he's a Claviger and I'm not, but I meant report it to Percy, I never meant you, you big ape!'

'Who's an ape? You're an ape,' said Savage. He had a talent for repartee.

'I still say you can't decide without Percy,' Garson argued. 'Not on an urgent matter, not without Percy.'

'Yes, we can,' Savage overruled him. 'It's an urgent matter. You're just after admitting it. Percy said we had to decide urgent matters for ourselves, it's important matters we're supposed to tell him.'

'But this is important,' Garson said. 'That's what I'm saying.'

'You're just after saying it was urgent. Is it urgent or is it important? Make up your mind, you can't have it both ways.'

Savage grinned in the anticipation of victory and called

out to the assembly, confusing them by the phrasing of his command.

'Hands up those who agree it's urgent.'

But before he could seize the victory he felt was within his grasp the troops were suddenly paralysed with fear. Someone was coming down the chute from the door in Tulip Place.

'It's Percy, it's Percy!' Frank Garson yelled in relief as a tall round-shouldered youth slouched into the range of the candlelight.

'What's going on here?' a mournful voice asked, a voice that had only recently been broken and sounded as if it was still being mended. 'I just thought yous was in here when I couldn't see a soul anywhere outside.'

Frank Garson rushed at him and clung to him.

'Help me, Percy! Save me! They're going to put me out of the Brotherhood. We were all out looking for you. We need you, Percy! We need you! Sheuch's trying to confuse me because I said it was urgent so he said we could decide it for ourselves but I said it was too important to decide without you, and he said I couldn't have it both ways, but if it's urgent it's important too, isn't it?'

Percy rocked on his toes and heels at the question and decided not to answer it.

'What were you putting him out for?' he asked, scowling round the meeting to remind them he had the seeing eye and they had better tell him the truth.

'Where'd ye get to?' Savage asked, boldly facing the seeing eye. 'We've been looking for you all night, so we have.'

'I was at a concert listening to a choir singing,' Percy answered in his faraway voice, his sad eyes dreamily focused on the furthest wall where the rats lived. 'It was rare, so it was. If we could get that piano there tuned I could start a choir with you lads if we could get somebody to play it.'

'That's just what I've been saying for years,' Savage agreed insolently.

'Scottish education, ach!' Percy snorted in bitterness.

'Percy, please!' Frank appealed to him, shaking his arm. But Percy was beyond his reach, mounted on his high horse again.

'They're supposed to learn you culture and how to live and they don't give you anything about philosophy or music. They never learn you how to write music for example. All they hammer into you is sums and spelling. If I could just read music I could form yous into a world-famous choir so I could. See the Vienna Boys' Choir?'

'No, where are they?' Savage asked eagerly, looking round the cellar with dramatic jerks of his head. 'Are they here the night?'

'They're only boys like you except that they speak German,' Percy explained, snubbing the Chief Claviger. For some time he had regretted ever appointing him. Savage seemed too coarse a type to do his job properly. 'But they've had a chance yous have never had because the Germans have always had a great love for music. The world's greatest composers are Germans like Batch and Baith-hoven.'

He rocked, toe to heel, heel to toe, dreaming how he would love to be the salvation of these poor neglected urchins by introducing them to the good things of life.

'Oh, Percy, listen!' Frank pleaded, clutching him, shaking him.

They were all clamouring at him, everybody shouting at once, demanding attention, trying to explain. He came sadly out of his dream. He gathered there was something worrying them. He submitted wearily to the duty of helping them and dismissed Savage from Miss Elginbrod's chair with a peremptory gesture and sat there himself. Nobody would ever say he shirked his duty. And he liked to sit where Miss Elginbrod used to sit. It was a kind of mild revenge. He put himself in the pose of Rodin's 'Thinker' as he had seen it on the cover of a book he got for sixpence on the barrows in Renfield Street, and waited patiently till his supreme position got silence. He liked silence even better than he liked music. That was why he didn't like his mother. She was always nattering.

'Gi' me a report,' he growled.

'Frank, Frank, Frank!' the Brotherhood chanted. 'He's the one that knows! Let him report!'

Savage huffed away from them, kicked a stack of old examination papers containing, though he didn't know it, his father's score of five out of forty in mental arithmetic thirty years ago.

'A frank report, eh?' Percy smiled down at them from his throne. 'Frank is always frank. That's what you call a pun, lads. I had nobody to tell me these things, that's why I like to tell you. Shakespeare was very fond of puns, and I like a good pun myself, so I do.'

'I like a pun too,' Savage muttered to the dusty sheets. 'A pun o' chocolates.'

Frank Garson went back to his place behind the lid of a dual desk, but this time without two warders holding him. He was the only child of a motor-mechanic who worked in the garage at the far end of Bethel Street, an intruder in a gang that respected his intelligence but distrusted his cleanliness. He seemed a cut above them because his father had a good job, and they couldn't understand why he was so keen to be a member, even ambitious to be a Claviger. It made them suspicious. But they all liked him in the end because he was always straight. His mother had deserted his father for a West Indian bus-driver four years ago, and he could remember her only dimly as a bright-eyed woman with comforting arms and a good kissing mouth. He remembered also a cosy smell, quite different from the smell of chalk that accompanied Miss Elginbrod. But he could never talk of his mother. A boy whose mother had run off with a coloured man inherited a shame, and the fact that he was clever, clean and loyal, and that his father was a non-smoker, non-drinker and churchgoer, merely made him more of an oddity to his mates. Their fathers were drunken, idle and cruel, but they knew their mothers just had to put up with it. What kind of a mother then had Frank Garson that ran away from a good husband? Frank knew she was condemned, and he carried her guilt always with him. Dark-haired, rosy-cheeked, innocent-faced, and well-spoken except when excitement made him stutter a little, he would have suited a choirboy's collar.

'The new janny,' he began, conquering his stutter in the hush that respected his report, 'he doesn't know where anything is, so he asked me to help him because the janny in Comelygrove asked him for the lend of the gipsy costumes we had in our school concert when your father was the janny because the Comelygrove are going to do a gipsy cantata at Christmas in the Bellfield Halls and he didn't know where they were but the janny in Comelygrove knew we had them all right, so the new janny asked me to look for them in the cellar because anything you can't find must be in the cellar he said. So I asked Jasper, that's the teacher that came when Miss Elginbrod retired, you've seen him, he comes here on a mo'bike and he's got big bushy eyebrows and a blue chin, that's what we call him, that or Bluebeard, but his right name's Whiffen, and he let me come down here at two o'clock to look for them and I came down through the basement, the janny opened the door for me and then left me, and I found them in the tea-chests over there.'

He stopped, his mouth working. He felt his stammer coming on, and he fought against it.

'End of Part One,' Savage called out from the rear. He put on a television advert voice and chanted as he performed a Red Indian war dance round the back and flanks of the assembly. 'Use the new super duper scientific formula automatic aw-tae-buggery Freezing Point. Never go without a Freezing Point. In a man's world a girl needs a Freezing Point. Washes whiter than black and prevents flavour blur. Get one now, get one tomorrow, get one last week. The time is out of joint till you get a Freezing Point. And now back to Maverick.'

'I think you've got far too much to say,' Percy reprimanded him severely. 'And stand still when the court's in session.'

'Well, tell him to get to the point then,' Savage answered shrilly.

'That's the point,' Frank hammered the desk, hating Savage. 'I found the c-costumes, Percy, and I found something else too, a lot more, in the tea-chests. I gave the c-costumes to the new janny but I didn't tell him what else I'd seen. I wasn't sure if I'd seen right so I told Specky. You see there was a big spider came scuttling down the side of the tea-chest when I took the costumes out and I got a fright.'

'Feart for a spider!' Savage commented in disgust. 'Feart for a spider and he wants to get a key one day! That's the kind of probationer you get nowadays. Before I could get into the gang at all I had to get the Chinese Rub and I had to break seven windows in the scheme and steal a hundred fags and—'

'I stopped all that,' Percy interrupted him, frowning at the mention of the barbarous rites used before he civilized the gang. 'That's nothing for boasting about. And I'm still waiting to hear what all the excitement's about.'

'I hit it with one of those shovels,' Frank explained, keeping his own course doggedly, 'and I knocked it on its end, the tea-chest I mean, and a lot of rubbish fell out, paper hats, you know, and decorations and that wand the fairy princess used and I saw a lot of money.'

'A spider, a big big spider,' Savage mimicked Frank's soprano. 'And he lost the heid. I wonder what he would have done if he'd saw one of the rats from the other end up there.'

'What do you mean, a lot of money?' Percy asked anxiously. There seemed no escape from dreams of money and talk of money.

'Pound notes and five-pound notes,' said Frank. 'I told Specky. And bags of silver, paper bags and cloth bags, you couldn't count it. I told Specky at playtime and we came down here after four by the door in the basement to make sure. I couldn't believe it, I thought maybe it was stage money, but there was too much of it. You couldn't spend it in years. You remember Miss Elginbrod put on a play about a millionaire that tried to give all his money away in an Alpine village but nobody would take it because they were happier without money. That's why I thought it was stage money at first. Then I wanted to tell the cops and Sheuch says I was going to break the law you gave us but I would have shared the reward with everybody here, honest I would, cross my throat and spit!'

He went through the actions in his excitement.

'But Specky said no, report it here,' he concluded, exhausted by his ordeal. 'He'll tell you that's how it was, you ask him!'

Specky rose from the coal-scuttle, bowed to Percy, turned and bowed to the Brotherhood and went into the witness-desk as willingly as Frank left it. He was going to enjoy this. He liked speaking. He would show them how a formal report ought to be made.

'Probationer Garson reported to me at afternoon interval,' he began benignly, 'that he had seen millions and millions of pounds under the costumes in the tea-chests. He requested me to accompany him in a further visit to procure verification. Immediately following the dismissal of afternoon school we therefore descended together to our present location via the door in the basement when the janny's back was turned and I personally inspected the receptacles indicated. I ascertained they contained money and I came to the conclusion that the money was genuine currency. However, I differed from Probationer Garson in my estimate of the amount. According to my calculations there are not millions and millions of pounds there at all. There are only—'

'I didn't mean millions and millions as millions,' Frank interrupted him resentfully, clenching his fists to keep his temper. 'I meant a lot, that was all.'

'At a tory estimate,' Specky proceeded, pleased at the chance to use a long-hoarded synonym, 'I would say there are only thousands of pounds dispersed in three of the six receptacles referred to.'

'What's the game?' Percy asked, wondering whether to be angry with them for trying to kid him or just laugh it off. 'What are yous up to now?'

'It isn't a game, Regent Supreme, sir,' Specky replied respectfully. 'It's true, I'm afraid. When I had made a provisional count of the contents of the first receptacle and then discovered that there was another two also containing money I abandoned the count and summoned an Extraordinary General Meeting in virtue of the powers vested in me as High Claviger. Chief Claviger Savage proposed immediate equal division of the money but I vetoed that in accordance with the constitution as laid by the Regent Supreme, that is yourself, sir.'

'You couldn't divide it,' Frank complained direct to Percy, appealing to him with his hands clasped in prayer. 'And even if you could you couldn't spend it. We'd be found out, bound to be! We'd all be in trouble. Please, Percy, tell the cops! Please!'

'I myself told Chief Claviger Savage equal division was out of the question,' Specky said with condescending calm to belittle Frank's hysteria, 'but he wouldn't agree. He even proposed to expel Probationer Garson for treason but I opposed that too and said it was a matter for the Regent.'

Percy bowed in regal acknowledgement. He was trying to think, and the chattering in front of him only confused him. There seemed to be something ominously true in what Frank and Specky were telling him, and in that case he must take charge and be cool, calm and collected. He mustn't get excited, and yet he felt his leg tremble under the weight of his elbow as he resumed his thinker's pose. The chattering became a clamour.

'Silence!' he shouted, in a temper with them.

'Permission to speak, please!' Skinny called out, his right hand high.

Percy grunted permission. He must keep patient and listen and try to think at the same time. It was difficult for him. Why was it, he wondered, that some folk were born with a quick brain, shrewd customers, fly men; and better

33

folk needed time and privacy to work things out? Where was the justice or equality in that? But he knew enough to know that silence can be mistaken for wisdom and that nothing is so infectious as panic. So he held his tongue and put on an air of indifference.

'The majority decision of the Clavigers was to refer the matter to you,' Skinny started, taking Specky's place behind the desk, 'because your father had charge of the cellar and you're your father's heir, so if the money in those chests belonged to your father then legally it's yours, and there was nobody else looked after the cellar, so it must have belonged to your father.'

'Ach, don't be daft, Skinny!' Frank shouted. 'You've seen what's there. Percy's father never had that kind of money, never, never, never!'

Skinny turned from addressing the chair to argue with his subordinate.

'How do you know? That's for Percy to say. Percy knows what his father had, you don't. Percy's the boss, it's no' you!'

'Well, I like that!' Frank screamed. 'It's me that's been arguing Percy's the boss, and now you try and tell me!'

Percy felt the first throbbings of a headache. It was the frequency of his headaches, beginning just after he left school, that made him suspect he was an intellectual. They were probably due to the abnormal activity of his brain.

'You've always said you should have had money if you had your rights,' Skinny turned back to the chair, 'so maybe this money is your inheritance, maybe that's why you could never find the money you knew your father ought to have left you if you were to be a great man because that's where he had hidden it.'

'Yes, could be,' said Percy, too overwhelmed to dispute the point. 'Let me see what yous are all talking about.'

He came clumsily down from Miss Elginbrod's chair and the Clavigers dragged the three lower tea-chests out of the darkness into the candlelight.

'That's how they were, with the three other chests on top

of them,' said Frank 'and there was all those costumes on top of the money but we put everything back just as it was to keep it hidden'.

Specky, Skinny and Savage pulled out concert costumes, Christmas party decorations and brown paper from the first chest, and Percy stooped over it when they gestured him to look inside. He fumbled out a bundle of notes with an elastic band round them and flipped it through with dumb awe.

'Those are all fivers,' said Frank helpfully. 'But there's singles as well there, and the bags with the half-crowns and the florins is in the middle one.'

Percy slouched round the other chests and examined them perfunctorily. The money was real. There was no doubt in his mind. And when the three chests were emptied of all the rubbish crammed in them to reveal the money underneath he saw that the bottom of each was covered with notes an inch deep. He felt slightly sick, much as he had felt when an old man in Packing and Dispatch had taken him into a pub and made him drink a pint of beer one night after they had been working late, and there was a quivering and a fluttering in his stomach.

'Cover it up again,' he said, stricken with responsibility. 'Hide it just as it was! And let me think! Let me think!'

'Oh no, Percy, no!' Frank whispered in dismay. He had seen the glint of greed, and he was afraid.

Percy ignored him, and the Clavigers hastily and willingly obeyed the order.

'Now put the chests well back, away back at that wall where the rats are,' Percy commanded firmly. 'We'll need time to think. I want to think about this.'

'But the rats might eat the money,' Skinny objected. 'It's only paper after all.'

'Some paper!' chuckled Savage.

'They'd have to eat their way through all those dresses and things first,' Specky commented, shrugging.

'And we'll be back before then!' Savage cried. He showed off his good young teeth like an animal showing its fangs as he leered in triumph at Frank Garson. 'Lovely lolly! All the lolly in the world there! And we'll be back!'

'Yes, we'll be back,' Percy admitted.

He felt a vague but none the less substantial right to the money. Even though he hadn't found it himself it had been found in his father's territory and he was his father's heir. Indeed, it had been his territory too. Many a Sunday he had been sent down to the cellar to look after the boilers in the days when the school was still heated by steam pipes. Many a Saturday he had spent sweeping it out and making it tidy before it became a neglected dump. It was merely accidental that someone else had found what was in those tea-chests. But the right didn't lie solely in the finding, it lay just as much in claim to the place. This cellar was his. He wondered where the money came from, but passed on at once. He had met somewhere in his grasshopper reading the remark that science consists in asking the right questions. That meant there were questions it was stupid to ask. For example, where this money came from. There was no answer. Why ask a question that couldn't be answered? The right question was what to do with it. But first he must frighten the Brotherhood into obedience.

'Gather round!' he yelled in his Regent's voice, and sat again in Miss Elginbrod's broken-backed chair.

'This is a very serious matter,' he declared. 'There'll have to be a solemn vow of secrecy. Yous have all got to swear not to say a word about it to anybody and take a blood oath.'

'That's the idea! Great!' Savage cried and rubbed his hands together and gloated.

Percy felt the glow of inspiration. It came to him sometimes when he was instructing the Brotherhood, a warm feeling round his brow and a tingling in his scalp, and he wished it would come oftener, it was so mysterious and thrilling. He took a safety-razor blade from his trouser-pocket, a blade he carried in a metal holder, and lightly and bravely he cut the ball of his thumb.

'Kneel before me one by one,' he commanded. 'And re-peat after me.'

They came to him in single file and he bent and dabbed the blood from his thumb on their forehead.

'I promise not to tell,' he incanted.

'I promise not to tell,' they repeated after him.

They waited in groups round the cellar after the oath had been taken, and then Percy told them they were all to come to a special meeting at eight o'clock the next evening, and they wouldn't lose by it. They left the cellar by the chute and scattered silently from Tulip Place. Percy ushered them out one by one and locked the door when they were all gone. He stayed there for a moment before hurrying down the chute and running over to the wall where the rats were supposed to be. He had never seen a rat there in his life. He dragged out one of the chests and whipped away the rub-bishy garments above the money.

Some of the notes were dirty, and some were fairly clean; some were creased and some had never been folded. He took a long time just looking at them, flipping them over and flipping them over but keeping each bundle in its elastic band. He noticed they were all from the same bank, but the numbers were all mixed up. It would be safe to pass them. He tried to work out just how much was there. If he counted what was in one chest and multiplied by three he might get a rough idea of the total. But Frank Garson was right. He couldn't count what was in one chest. He kept on losing the place. He would need a bit of paper to write on and keep the score. He attacked the bundle of fivers and tried to do it by short methods: twenty in each bundle was a hundred and ten bundles were a thousand. But when he came to count fifteen, sixteen and seventeen bundles he wasn't sure if seventeen meant the bundle he had just counted or the one he was just going to count. He gave in and gave it up. He knelt over the chest, his arms thrown across it and his head on his arms, and he wept.

He could have coped with buried Inca treasure and found delight in a sunken galleon or a pirate hoard. He could have revelled in plundering an Egyptian tomb and taken the jewels of Ophir in his stride. Gold in Arizona or diamonds from Africa would have been a thrill within his range. But so much ready wealth in the commonplace form of pound notes and five-pound notes frightened him. It was too stark, too simple, too easy. He knew it was too much as well, but it was his. Not for a moment did he think otherwise, even as tears rolled down his cheeks where a fine floss still waited its first shearing.

'Oh, God help me!' he moaned. 'Please, God! Help me!'

CHAPTER FOUR

The special meeting was a nervous, frightened affair. Even Savage was slightly scared. Percy spoke so long and so mournfully on the dangers and responsibilities of their position, his brooding eyes seeming to see right into their trembling souls, that he gave them all the jitters. At one point they would mostly have settled gladly for five bob if that would let them out of it, but then he spoke of the freedom before them if they were obedient and faithful, and they saw a lifetime of happiness ahead.

'Now, to avoid any suspicion and to make sure yous are not found out,' he said, 'I'm only going to allow yous a little at a time, and yous'll get it only for a particular purpose, something you want right away, and you'll tell me what it is, otherwise you won't get it, so that nobody'll ever find you with a lot of money on you. Now, I can't always be watching yous, and there's three of you got a key to the side door and any of yous could slip down through the basement during school hours if you were willing to take the risk of being caught by the janitor, so we'll make a gentlemen's agreement to do it my way and never go behind my back to take any of it on your own.'

He explained a gentlemen's agreement to them, and to begin with he limited them to the silver. It kept them from buying anything big enough to arouse comment from the gossips at the close-mouth in the tenements round about, and it kept the younger members happy enough. A couple of half-crowns was wealth to them. But he knew he was only postponing the problem of what to do about the folding money. He heard a murmuring against him in the higher ranks of the Brotherhood. Skinny supported him, but Savage was niggling and Specky was slippery.

'Ah, but look,' Skinny argued when Savage wanted to remove the paper money in handfuls, 'we made a gentlemen's agreement. You can't break a gentlemen's agreement, that's the whole point about a gentlemen's agreement, you can't break it, that's why Percy made us make it. Percy's right, you know, Percy's shrewd.'

'To hell with Percy!' Savage spat.

'You'd only spoil everything any other way,' said Specky. 'I hate to admit it, but you've got to. But what he ought to do is give us more or put one of the chests aside for us and nobody else.'

'Gentlemen's agreement!' cried Savage. 'Where's the gentlemen? Him, he's only a janny's son. Mind you, my old man's a gentleman all right, he hasn't worked for fifteen year. Us three could empty those chests in a week. We could stash it somewhere else. We're the only ones with a key, we could slip in any time at all. Nobody would know.'

'Percy would know,' Specky pointed out so quickly that Savage saw he had thought of it himself already. 'Then the rest of them would get to know and they'd start coming in through the door in the basement.'

'And if you make it a free-for-all you'll only get us all caught,' Skinny complained. 'Somebody would clype. I bet you wee Garry would go to the cops. It's only because Percy's took charge that he's keeping quiet. Oh, he loves Percy! He thinks Percy's wonderful! Take away Percy and it would be a disaster. Garry would shop us in an hour.'

'I'm afraid that's right,' Specky conceded sadly. 'You've

got to keep the agreement, for a bit anyway. Percy's right enough in a way. Ye canny give pound notes to folk like Pinkie and wee Noddy and Cuddy.'

'What could they buy?' Skinny asked earnestly. 'If they started spending big money where could they put whatever they bought? Folk would be bound to notice. What could Noddy put in a single-end for example?'

'Him?' said Savage flippantly. 'He's that stupit he'd buy a grand piano and try and hide it under the kitchen sink. He's real daft about music. Give him a tune he's never heard before and he'll play it for you right off on the mouth-organ.'

'He's got a super one now all right,' Skinny remarked. 'Made in Germany. He got one made in Germany because Percy said the Germans were the best in the world at music like the Spaniards at football.'

'Percy patted him on the head when he said what he was going to buy with his ration and told him he was a very wise boy for putting it to a good use,' Specky said, and shook his head at the memory.

'Ach, The Rangers could beat them any time,' Savage bridled.

'Don't talk wet,' said Specky. 'They never even qualified to meet Real Madrid, sure Eintracht slaughtered them.'

'They were lucky,' Savage said, and waved his hands in front of Specky's face to wave the topic away. 'A ten-bob mouth-organ's all right for Noddy, but I want mair nor that. I want ready cash in my pocket.'

'Aye, it would be rare,' Skinny said.

'Instead of this percy-monious weekly ration,' Specky said brightly, looking round for a laugh but the word was unknown to his comrades, and he sighed at the company he had to keep.

Percy was worried. He knew what they were thinking, he could guess what they were saying. He slept badly, wondering how to control them, and the solution came to him in disturbed dreams. But he didn't tell them he had dreamt of the solution, he told them that what he had to do was revealed to him in a dream. Maybe it was because his mother had laughed at him for comparing himself to Moses, but he had a dream about Moses and found help in it. He dreamt he was on a mountain top and the clouds were all around him and he couldn't see anything but a grey mist that chilled him to the bone. Then suddenly the mist was gone and there was a risen sun and everything was made clear to him though he couldn't put it into words. He went down to the plain by a winding stony path, running sure-footed like a mountain goat, full of zest for the new way of life revealed to him. He found the Brotherhood anxiously awaiting him and he raised his hand and blessed them and they were sheep and he was their shepherd, and somehow he was holding a crook in his hand though he hadn't been holding one before.

A sheer coincidence gave substance to his vague dream. Turning the pages of the same dictionary where he had found that claviger meant a keyholder he saw the word 'bethel' and stopped at it because it was the name of the street where he lived. The dictionary said that bethel meant a Methodist church and came from the Hebrew *Beth-El*, the House of God. The discovery set him trembling with excitement, for he knew that as a poet he must believe in the magic of words, and it came to him in a flash of inspiration that El wasn't only the God of the Hebrews, it was also in one of its forms the sign for the pound note. It was more than a coincidence to him. It had a meaning. It was a revelation, completing the revelation of his dream. The street called the House of God contained the cellar that contained the pound notes, and the pound notes were El and he was the prophet of El just as much as Moses was. He felt the burden of the elect upon him.

He intimidated the Brotherhood by the force of his will for power over them, by the nagging of his cracked voice, by the solemnity of his face. He gathered them in the cellar and spoke to them like a preacher.

'Yous has all been poor neglected boys all your life, without a good suit to your name or a good pair of shoes, but

God has a special care for the poor and underprivileged, and sometimes He reveals Himself to them, like He done to the Jews. He chose the Jews and that's what He's did to you, He's chose you to get the good of this manna from Heaven to help you in the desert, 'cause you see this life is like a desert. He chose you, He didn't choose boys from Govan or the Gorbals or Maryhill or Partick or Whiteinch, no, He chose you. Just think about that. Just think what that means. It might have been anybody and it was yous. Now that proves you are the chosen people, only you need a lawman like the Jews had Moses. Well, I'm your lawman, and you have got to do like I say or else.'

He believed they had been chosen because he believed he had been chosen, and they had to believe it too. There was a halo round his head, a vision in his eyes, authority in his voice. They were only children, he frightened them – especially when he threatened what would happen if they committed the sin of disobedience. The youngest weren't sure if he meant they would go to hell for ever or go to jail for ever. He made them all take a new and more elaborate blood oath, and when they had taken it they had to make the sign of the El. He showed them how to do it. They drew the index finger of the right hand across the eyes from left to right, up over the brow in a loop, and down the line of the nose to the chin. Then they traced another loop to the left and came back along the jawbone and up to the right ear. The sign was completed by drawing two parallel lines across the tip of the nose and upper lip. It was the sign of the £ drawn on their face, the symbol of the god they were now to serve.

He had written the oath on a little card he held in his hand, with a bar between the phrases to keep him right as he read it out.

'Repeat after me,' he said, and they repeated the phrases.

'I solemnly swear – I solemnly swear – not to reveal – not to reveal – the place of the treasure – the place of the treasure – to anybody – to anybody – and I solemnly swear – and I solemnly swear – not to speak of the treasure – not to speak of the treasure – outside this cellar – outside this cellar – nor to touch the treasure – nor to touch the treasure – without permission – without permission – of the Regent Supreme – of the Regent Supreme.'

They took the oath standing. When they knelt down he said the rest for them, making it sound more frightening than they could ever have managed in their own unguided treble.

'And if I break this oath may the Brotherhood break the bones of my thighs. If I speak of the treasure outside the cellar let my tongue be burnt with a soldering iron, and if I touch the treasure without the Regent's permission may the hand that commits the offence be eaten by the rats in the cellar and may my arms be paralysed, withered and shrivelled till they drop off like a dead leaf from the trees in autumn.'

He made the Clavigers take the same oath, to remind them that they were his subordinates and they too could touch the money only with his permission.

Zealous, sincere and worried, oppressed by his responsibility for them and for so much money, he never thought what he himself might do with it. He was too busy driving them far beyond a mere gentlemen's agreement, imposing on them a religious attitude, a true piety, towards the uncounted wealth.

He was surprised how quickly and easily he got it all going the way he wanted. He declared the word 'money' tabu. They were never to use it to say what was in the cellar. They were to say 'El'. He told them it was the only safe word to use. The other word would give away their secret and bring a terrible punishment. He said they would all get scabies, chickenpox, dysentery and measles if they ever used it.

Savage was just as frightened as the rest of them by Percy's talk, but he couldn't entirely conquer his natural flippancy, even for blood oaths, candlelight, hymn-singing and bell-ringing. Halfway through one of Percy's early sermons on the almighty power of El he nudged Specky

and whispered, giggling, 'If you want anything, go to El!'
He chanted audibly a counting-out rhyme used by Glasgow
children, an obscure rhyme from an unknown source, supposed by local antiquaries to be of Druidic origin.

> *El, El, Domin – El,*
> *Eenty, teenty, figgerty – fel!*

Percy heard him and was shocked. He knew there was
danger to them all in irreverence. Their secret would be
safe only if he could make them appreciate the sacredness
of what they had found. They must be made to understand
that the finding of the money imposed a great piety on
them. He must bind them to an unquestioning respect for
himself as the person who had first led them to the land
where El had appeared to them. They must have faith.
They must be made to see it was a divine revelation, and
they must obey him as its medium.

He thought of expelling Savage, but he was afraid it
might make him an enemy, a spiteful Ishmael who would
go to the pagan world outside the cellar with a story of
hidden treasure and come back with a band of freebooters
to invade the sanctuary of El. The fear of it kept him awake
at night, fretting. It was no joke being in charge of a crowd
of children. So he spoke to Savage privately and told him it
was a matter of policy to make the Brotherhood respect the
holy name of El. If they didn't, it would mean complete
lawlessness and nobody would win. They would all lose
everything.

'Aye, I see fine what you're after,' Savage answered, and
grinned with an atheist's insolence at the gangling Regent.
'You're right enough. You're a fly big bugger, aren't you?
It's the only way to keep these stupid bastards in order. But
you don't expect me to believe all that tripe about El reveal-
ing himself to us because we're a chosen people, now do
you?'

'Why not?' Percy asked coldly. 'I believe in El, why
shouldn't you? You think you're too clever maybe? Let me

tell you, there are more things in Heaven and earth than are dreamt of in your philosophy, Horace. And just let me warn you, you'd better believe in El in front of the Brotherhood or I'll cut you off from El altogether.'

He made them make the sign of the El at every meeting and rang the bell three times before they filed forward for their weekly allowance. Inspired by his position as their guide, philospher and friend he made up a hymn for them to the tune of *The Ash Grove*, careful to work in his own name as an essential item in what he called the 'relevation' of El.

'Down, down in our cellar, where rubbish concealed him,
When daylight is fading, we bow unto El,
And promise to follow the one who revealed him.
So sing Percy's praises and ring out the bell.'

After that they chanted with gusto to the tune of *Boney Was a Warrior*, 'El is our salva-ti-on, rah, rah, rah!' They particularly enjoyed the 'rah, rah, rah' bit, and Percy was thrilled to have a choir of his own even if it wasn't just as good as the Vienna Boys'.

For nearly a month he lived more delighted with the success of converting the gang into a reverent congregation than with his lordship over the money. He was proving himself a poet at last. He was a sacred bard whose job it was to create and maintain the religious secrets of his tribe. All he bought for himself was a plush-covered copy of Shelley's poems, and a portable typewriter to type his own poems for publication ónce he got them written down. Later on he could get whatever else he wanted, there was always tomorrow. Meanwhile he kept the Brotherhood in order, he accepted only reasonable demands for money, and he advised them how to spend what they asked for. Still excited with the miracle performed for them, the boys didn't think of asking for much. Like Percy they found their satisfaction in dreaming of the future, when they could have whatever they wanted. Like him, they enjoyed the secrecy and the mystery of it, they loved the hymn-singing and the bell-ringing in candlelight, the sense of belonging to a chosen people when they made the sign of the El. It was better than going to church. They could understand it. They could see what they were asked to adore and they felt it concerned them and the real world they lived in. The Clavigers stopped murmuring and bided their time.

'Ach he's out of this world altogether,' Specky said pityingly. 'He's round the bend. He's carrying on like a real Holy Willie.'

'Aye, he's round the bend all right,' Skinny agreed sadly. 'Do you know I don't think he's touched a penny of it for himself.'

'No, just a few fivers,' said Savage. 'There are nae pennies in it. Nothing so common. I bet he's been shifting it in wads every night in the week when we're no' there.'

'Oh, I don't believe that,' Specky said reproachfully.

'How would we know if he wasn't?' Savage demanded. 'Tell me that and tell me no more. Don't forget it was never counted. To this day it hasna been counted. He could dae what he likes wi' it. He could tell us in another month it was all done, and we couldn't argue. Ye know, he had a bloody cheek making us give him back our keys. Clavigers! He likes big words. I bet ye he likes big money too.'

'Well, after all it was him that gave them to us.' Skinny said. 'They were his to start with. It was him got them cut from the key his old man had.'

'You know, I could apply my boot to my posterior,' said Specky. 'I should have got one cut before I gave him mine back. I should have anticipated some such manoeuvre on his behalf.'

'You mean you didn't expect him to do that?' Savage asked, and grinned, his animal teeth on a victory parade.

Unable to resist showing off he thrust his hand into the back pocket of his tight studded jeans and showed them a new key.

'I thought of it all right,' he boasted. 'I used the loaf. It's time you brushed up your IQ, Specky.'

'You can't brush up an IQ,' Specky tutted at him. 'An IQ is the result of the primitive formation of your inherited characteristics from your paw and your maw. You can't do a thing about it.'

'Well, you could dust your brains then, couldn't you?' Savage retorted, shoving the key away in his back pocket again. He was content to wait. He had a key. He had the whip hand.

CHAPTER FIVE

The silver was done. There wasn't a half-crown or a florin left. They had all been squandered on sweeties, cigarettes, lemonade, playing cards, slot-machines, comics and the pictures. Percy burned the pokes and faced at last the problem of what to do about the folding money. He thought of changing handfuls of notes into silver and keeping the gang going a little longer on a diet of half-crowns, but he was nervous about going into a bank with the notes in case he was asked questions, and to go round the local shops, changing singles and fivers here and there, would only cause talk. Anyway, he saw he couldn't keep them much longer from real spending. They were all getting peevish with him. He made up his mind to start them off on pound notes. He thought he could trust them, but he warned them just the same.

'Yous don't want to look too affluential,' he addressed them from the chair in the candlelight. 'And you shouldn't buy anything conspicious. You have got to be very careful from now on.'

'A fine thing if we've got the money and canny spend it,' Savage commented at the foot of the throne.

'Of course you can spend it,' Percy scolded him, resenting the comment. 'There's nothing to prevent you from spending it if you want to spend it. All I'm saying is you've got to be careful and don't spend it on things that would get you asked awkward questions. Yous want to detract attention from yourselves.'

'And just buy sweeties like?' Specky asked. 'Boy-oh-boy! Twenty shillings' worth of lollipops! Nobody would ever dream of asking what you were doing with all those lollipops, not much.'

It was beginning to dawn on him, as on some of the others, that there wasn't much they could do with so much money. They would be better off with less. It would be easier to spend.

'Don't be funny,' Percy snapped at him. 'It takes brains to be funny. And you fellows should be helping me, you're the Clavigers, not niggling and nattering and trying to be sarky. I don't like folk that are sarky, and I don't like folk that nag.'

He gave out the pound notes grudgingly and hoped for the best. In a little while he found they weren't spending them, they were accumulating them and little groups were pooling their resources for purposes they kept secret from him. They began to demand a twice-weekly ration, and he gave in to them for the sake of peace. He was in the cellar every night to satisfy himself everything was all right. Then various members of the Brotherhood began to turn up every night too and tap at the side-door till he had to let them in. Once they were in he had to let them have something before they would go away. He felt he had lost the place somewhere, but he didn't see what he could do about it.

He gave up his job without telling his mother and spent his days at the Mitchell Library pursuing an elusive something he thought of as his studies. He looked particularly for books in one volume that would tell him what he wanted to know. He read Wells' *Outline of History* in a hop, skip, and jump, and from Russell's *History of Western Philosophy* he wrote out the names of the philosophers. He made notes on what he tried to read, haphazard notes, not always coherent or legible, but still notes. It made him feel more like a real student when he sat in the Mitchell Library and took notes. Odd items of information stuck to him, items as dead and separate as flies on flypaper, but for all that he was learning. Sometimes his eyes ached and he wondered if glasses would make him look more like a student or if he wouldn't suit them.

It was a great pleasure to him to sit amongst the under-graduates and look at the legs of the girls from Queen Margaret College when they sat across from him with their knees crossed. It made him feel he was a student too. He went home every day at the usual time after a cheap lunch in a small back-room restaurant near Charing Cross, and every week he took the amount of his wages from one of the tea-chests and handed it over to his mother. Some-times he thought of buying her a present or making her a gift of a hundred pounds or so, but he always decided not to bother. In the first place, she didn't deserve it, the way she was always finding fault with him, and in the second place she would only ask questions, not scientific ones, but the wrong ones, like where did you get all that money. He admired himself for not having given up his job at once. It proved his consideration for others. He had been so busy getting the Brotherhood organized under the protection of El that he hadn't had time to think of himself.

'I suppose some folk would say I should get my head examined,' he said to himself proudly, scratching it. 'But worldly matters are beneath we poets.'

The thought reminded him he had meant to write poetry if ever he had time. He bought a beautiful big book, half-bound in leather, like a ledger except that it wasn't ruled off for cash entries, and he meant to start writing poetry in it. But he had to hide it from his mother, and that made it hard for him to get a chance to write in it. He didn't seem to have any time at all to himself, even though he wasn't working. The Brotherhood found employment for him. They made him their errand-boy: because of his age it was he who had to go into town and buy what they wanted.

They were quite changed from the weeks when a pocketful of silver was enough for them. They outflanked him: they didn't want the money as money, they wanted things. And he had to go and get them.

'We could buy a ball and strips and start a team,' said Cuddy. 'The Brotherhood Rangers. The Bethel Thistle, eh? A dark blue jersey with an orange lily.'

'Is that all you can think of?' Percy cried, despairing of his chosen people. 'Football! Can you no' think of anything else but football? Do you never think of culture? You could buy Shakespeare's plays or a season ticket for the SNO. And who would you play? Tell me that! There's no league for a street team for lads of your age, and folk would ask where you got the money for a strip.'

'That's all you can say,' Noddy complained. 'Whatever we want to buy you say folk'll ask questions, that's what you keep saying. Have we no' to buy anything?'

In the end Percy went into town and bought them a strip. He bought them two strips, and three balls, and two dozen pair of football boots. But they never wore the strips or the boots except at night in the cellar, when they played a brawling game of five-a-side. Percy kept the jerseys, pants and stockings in his own house every day, telling his mother they were the strip of the school football team (the school hadn't a team), and he was their trainer.

In a big shop in Renfield Street he bought a ukelele one week and a guitar the next because Noddy insisted money ought to be spent on his musical education. He took a bus to Shawlands one afternoon and bought a tape-recorder because somebody thought it would be fun to have one, and another afternoon he went across the river to Maryhill for a transistor set, and while he was there he bought himself an electric razor. It was high time he was shaving every day. He told his mother the foreman had got it as a Christmas present, didn't like it and gave it to him for nothing. He had to tell her something. He couldn't go into hiding every time he wanted to shave. Another day he went over to Govan and bought a record-player. Much of the stuff he was sent to buy wasn't meant to be anyone's particular property. The tape-recorder, the record-player, the transistor, the television were everybody's and nobody's. They were bought because of a general will for them, and they furnished the cellar as a club for the Brotherhood. They were kept in the cellar and used there and nowhere else. The electricity required was got by using an adapter plug in one of the light-sockets. These items were not only kept in the cellar, they had to be hidden in case the janitor came across them, and Percy lost sleep worrying they would be found in spite of all his precautions. He worried too when he saw every member of the Brotherhood wearing a wristlet watch. Some of them had a pocket-watch as well, and he was sure they would attract attention. They had cameras too, Leicas and Voigtländers and Zeiss Ikons, but they didn't dare use them.

Friday nights were a great comfort to him. He had been beaten in his attempt to limit the spending of the money but he was determined not to yield on the Friday night service. He was grateful nobody opposed him. It was quite the opposite. In their orgy of spending they seemed to enjoy the Friday night with more zest and reverence than they had shown when he had sent them away with five bob each. They weren't just obeying him from force of habit, or doing casually what they knew he wanted done. They were doing it because they wanted to. They had taken over his creed and ritual and made them their own.

By their very submission to him they corrupted him, like a country that by accepting a dictator gives him a legal authority and wider scope for fanaticism. He had set out to be their leader, and he had become their slave, and he followed the code of his masters. He wakened to wants he had never known when he was only a packer in the Coop in Nelson Street. If his boys could find things to buy, then so should he to keep up with them. He bought a leather pocket-book so as to have something to carry pound notes and fivers in, for although he rationed the Brotherhood he never went out without twenty pounds in his pocket. He bought binoculars that cost him forty pounds, two expensive fountain pens to write his poems with and a dictionary of quotations to give him a short cut to a knowledge of English poetry. Lying in bed one night he had foreboding he might have to leave in a hurry and travel far in search of peace and quiet, so he bought a big briefcase, in genuine pigskin, and hid it in the cellar against the rats' wall. It had three compartments and he kept a suit of pyjamas and his shaving tackle, carefully wrapped, in one compartment. The other two would hold thousands, he was sure. He bought a pair of skates and went to the ice-skating at Crossmyloof, more to see the pretty girls there, and try to pick up one of them, than because he was keen on skating. He bought a fishing-rod and basket, and boots and waders and a jacket and hat to match, though he knew nothing about fishing and didn't know where to go fishing anyway. But he had read that fishing was a solitary and peaceful sport, fit for thoughtful men, and he hoped he would find time to be solitary and peaceful some day.

He bought himself a new suit after he stopped working because he believed a gentleman of leisure should be well-dressed, and when his mother made a scene about it he said he had been saving up for it for a year. She snorted sceptically and said no more, so he bought another couple of suits and shirts and ties to go with them. If he was smart and well dressed he might have a better chance of getting a girl, and a poet whose life was dedicated to the pursuit of beauty shouldn't be wearing shabby clothes.

Seeing Jasper's motor-bike parked in the blind-alley aroused him to a new want. Why shouldn't he have one too? He bought one. After all, Shelley had a boat. A poet must move with the times, and Shelley would certainly have had a motor-bike or a racing-car if he was alive today. What's more, he would probably have written an ode to Speed. He began one himself, just to do what Shelley would have done, and wrote the first three lines in his leather-bound log-book.

O wild Speed, be thou me, impetuous one,
Driving my thoughts around the universe,
And let the engine of my spirit run . . .

He didn't know where or how he wanted his spirit to run, so he left it till he could get peace and quiet to finish it.

Meanwhile he was busy learning to ride the bike. He had a skidlid and L-plates and a manual, and Frank Garson's father gave him a few tips. He parked it in the blind-alley every night, at the same spot as Jasper's bike was parked during the day from nine to four.

'How do you come to be having a motor-bike?' his mother asked.

'I won it in a raffle,' he said, very short with her.

She looked at him with her mouth hanging open. She was used to his being insolent and sarcastic to her, and she wouldn't give him the satisfaction of arguing when he gave silly answers to serious questions. But this one sounded so casual it might well be the truth. But it couldn't be true, for it was clearly absurd. She was baffled to silence.

He was parking the bike in Tulip Place one Thursday night at half past ten, before it was quite dark, after a thrilling practice run to Balloch and the banks of Loch Lomond, when a man came out of the close across the street and jabbed a finger in the small of his back. Percy jumped. In a moment's searing intuition he saw the hoard discovered, the owner identified, and himself in jail. The early summer evening seemed no longer beautiful, but ominous, and the sun he had seen setting behind the Campsies was a signal of the doom he had come back to meet.

'D'ye know Mr Phinn?' the stranger whispered, his scrubby face close against Percy's smooth chin. The electric razor was doing a very efficient job.

'Mr Phinn?' Percy asked hoarsely.

'Mr Phinn,' the stranger said, nodding his head like a hand-puppet.

Percy was frightened. He didn't see a square man in a belted raincoat, stained and shabby, with a curly-brimmed felt hat down over his eyes and a scar from the wing of his nose to the bend of his right jawbone. This was no Glasgow bauchle. What he saw was a looming supernatural figure that he identified with a deity he thought of as Nimeesis.

'Well, I'm Phinn,' he said cautiously. 'Percy Phinn. You see, I'm named after Percy Shelley the poet. You don't mean me, do you?'

He didn't think anyone would ever think of him as Mr Phinn, any more than you would think of Shelley as Mr Shelley, and he was puzzled. But with him that was the same thing as being frightened. The stranger shook his head, the horizontal movement as puppet-like as the vertical one had been.

'No,' he breathed vigorously into Percy's face, and Percy recognized the smell of whisky. His father used to drink that stuff. With the speed of lightning, for thought is swift even in the slowest, he wondered if it would be worthwhile buying a bottle of whisky to find out what it was like, decided a bottle of wine would be a more appropriate drink for a poet, regretted he had never thought of buying a bottle of wine for communal wine-drinking at the Friday Night Service, feared his buying days were over, and simultaneously found an answer to the stranger.

'Well, I'm Mr Phinn if you like,' he offered, prepared to sacrifice himself to save his boys.

'I don't like,' said the stranger.

'Ye'll jist have to like it I'm afraid,' Percy said bravely, but he felt his belly trembling and his left leg was quivering, 'there's no other Phinn about here. What Mr Phinn do you mean?'

'Who's the janitor in that school there?' the stranger asked, and thrust his head towards the building behind Percy.

'Oh, you mean him?' said Percy, and sagged in relief. Nobody could question the dead. 'That was my father so it was. Is that who you mean?'

'Well, what do you mean there's no Mr Phinn here?' the stranger demanded irritably. 'Has he been shifted? You're after saying your father's here. Do you mean he's been shifted?'

'No, he's no' been shifted, but he's no' here now,' Percy said brightly. 'He's dead.'

'Are you kidding?' the stranger whispered, his face so close to Percy's that they looked like two Eskimoes making love.

'What would I be kidding for?' Percy answered indignantly. 'I wouldn't be kidding about a thing like that, would I? I can show you his grave if you don't believe me.'

'Oh Jesus Christ!' said the stranger and bowed his head in grief.

Percy was impressed by the piety of the ejaculation.

'Did you know my father?' he asked tenderly.

They stood looking at each other under the single gas-lamp in the drab lonely alley called Tulip Place by a poetic Town Council, and the summer twilight gathered into darkness.

'Naw, I never knew him,' said the stranger impatiently, then slowed to a fonder utterance. 'Och aye, I knew him well.'

'I see,' said Percy uneasily.

'You see that door there, does that door lead to a cellar?' the stranger asked, jabbing a finger abruptly at the scarred door across the pavement.

'Oh aye, that was for the coal,' said Percy. 'But it's never used now.'

'You've got a key for it, have you no'?' the stranger said with a smile so ingratiating that it put Percy in a new panic.

'Oh no,' he disclaimed hastily. 'That door's never used now, it was for the coal you see, but you see they don't use the boilers now, cause it's all electric, so there's no key for it, ye canna get in that way at all, it's no' a door really, it's all bricked up inside, so you see a key's no use. Because of the bricks. Ye canna get in that way. It's all bricked up.'

'You mean it's bricked up?' the stranger glowered. 'Then how do you get in? Tell me that!'

'Well, there's a door in the basement,' Percy admitted, 'in the school I mean, but it's never used, you see, and nobody's got a key to it. You see it's no' a cellar now, it's just a rubbish dump and nobody has ever any call to go in there, and it's overrun wi' rats, you see.'

'I see,' the stranger said patiently. 'Did your father ever mention any of his pals to you, doing a favour for them like, you know? Did you know your Uncle Sammy?'

Before Percy could decide on the best answer they heard someone plodding along Bethel Street. They turned together in alarm and looked at the corner. A policeman was passing on patrol. Percy knew him. It was Constable Knox, the local bobby who had often taken a wee rest in the cellar in the old days and had a cup of tea with his father. He raised a hand in greeting as Constable Knox passed and the policeman acknowledged it with a nod so dignified it was almost imperceptible. Then when he turned again to cope with the stranger Percy found he was alone. He was just in time to catch a glimmer of a raincoat scurrying through the close on the other side of Tulip Place. He set his motor-bike safely against the kerb and galloped home on a wild bronco of alarm.

CHAPTER SIX

He made quite sure the stranger wasn't in Tulip Place or Bethel Street the following night before he went down to the cellar by the side door. He was glad it was a Friday night, for that meant every member of the Brotherhood would be present to attend the Friday Night Service. He had taught them to refer to it as the FNS, and they were drilled to accept the penalty of forfeiting a week's money if they missed it. He let them in cautiously, opening the door no wider than was needed to admit a sidling entrance, and after the Creed and the hymn, before they came forward in single file for the share-out, he made a little speech. It was understood that any announcements he had to make would be made between the singing of the hymn and the distribution of the grace of El, so when the choir had finished the hymn and the campanologist had rung the bell three times to emphasize the end of that part of the service, he stood before Miss Elginbrod's chair and addressed them solemnly with the scarf of a Rangers' supporter draped round his shoulders like a stole.

'I've got an important announcement to let yous know,' he said, and looked from left to right and back to front before going on. He had read that a pause could be used with great effect in public speaking, a pause and a look, so he paused and he looked. There was silence. Gratified by the hush he went on. 'The holy sanctuary of El is in danger from the prying nose of a stranger. An enemy. Yous all know that in this world which is a vale of tears we are continuously besieged by enemies seeking for to devour us. El is ours and we are El's and it's our duty to behave so as to keep it that way. Now you have got to be told that just the other night, not far from this place where we meet to pay our respects to El, I was detained by a man who was certainly a spy sent here by them we've got to beware of. He proclaimed for to have knew my father but he made a strong depression on me of having an interest in how to get in here. So if yous ever see a bowly-legged man anywhere in Tulip Place or Bethel Street yous is not to knock at the door. Wait till he goes away. And if he doesn't go away don't come anywhere near the door. He only wants to find the way in, and if he ever does we've all had it. You know what happened to the Incas of Peru when the Spaniards discovered Montezuma's treasure.'

They didn't, but the way he said it made them understand it wasn't a good thing for Montezuma.

Savage lurched from squatting at the right foot of the Regent Supreme, bowed insolently to the Brotherhood, and turned half-right to speak to the chair.

'What should we no' come in by the door in the basement then for?' he asked. 'There's nobody could see us that way if we came in through the playground and went down to the basement.'

'Of course you would be seen,' Percy said impatiently. 'Yous would have to go in by the main gate, wouldn't you? And yous would have to cross the playground right in front of the janny's house. He'd be bound to see you. It's no' dark till after eleven o'clock these nights. Or else he'd hear you. I know. I lived there long enough. Just take my word for it if you don't believe me. And anyway the door in the basement's kept locked. The new janny keeps it locked. And I never managed to get a key for it. So you see you just couldna get in that way. And even if you could you would never manage it, no' without getting caught.'

'Aw, I see,' said Savage, and squatted with such a pleased smile that Percy was puzzled. And being puzzled he worried.

But it was time to go on with the business of the evening and he let Savage rest. He stood before the first of the three tea-chests, signalled the campanologist by making the sign of El in mid-air, and when the bell had been rung the Brotherhood came forward to the chest and knelt down to whisper their request.

'Four fivers,' said Noddy, making the required sign on his brow as he humbly knelt at Percy's large crepe-soled shoes.

Percy frowned. How quickly times had changed since they were content to ask for a small sum for a particular purpose! Now they asked for an absurd amount and never thought of telling him what they wanted it for. They had panted through an orgy of spending, asking for things instead of money. And he had agreed. He had even been their errand-boy. That was his mistake. He saw it too late, and stood frowning at Noddy in disapproval. This was a new phase. They had tired of buying things they couldn't use and couldn't hide. Now they wanted money again, not for anything special but just to have the money itself as power in their pocket. He had given in to them too long, he had let the gentlemen's agreement lapse. It was high time he made a stand.

'No,' he said firmly. 'That's far too-too much for you. You just want it. You don't want it for anything.'

'I do,' said Noddy. 'I'm saving up for a piano.'

'And where would you put a piano if you had one?' Percy demanded. 'You'd have the whole street talking. You'll get one, and like it.'

'One fiver,' said Noddy humbly.

'One single,' said Percy meanly, and handed him it.

Noddy took the pound without arguing, but he muttered behind Percy's back. Savage listened to him. Savage courted him.

'Are you saving up hard?' he asked Noddy on the stairs the next morning. They lived up the same close.

Noddy nodded. He wasn't given to saying much.

'It'll take you a long time to get enough for a piano at Percy's rate,' he suggested.

'Aye, so it will,' said Noddy neutrally.

'And if ye're saving up what are you doing for spending-money?' Savage asked sympathetically.

Noddy brought his shoulders up to his ears and showed off two black-palmed hands. He said nothing to mean nothing.

'Here I'll give you a few bob for spending,' Savage said, lording it over the dumb urchin, and gave him two ten-shilling notes. 'Percy isn't the only prophet of the great god El, ye know. Just you see me tonight at seven outside the pictures and I'll give you something to help to get your piano.'

He gave him twenty pounds. He had been entering the cellar secretly at midnight for a week past and taking away money in handfuls from the third and last of the tea-chests, the one that was stowed away in the farthest corner of the rat-wall, the chest Percy seemed to think would do for their old age. Some of the money he hid up the chimney in the back room of his house, where a gas-fire had been fitted into the place once filled by the cradle for a coal fire. Some of it he hid inside the derelict air-raid shelter, built before he was born and never pulled down, that filled the hinterland of the tenement where he lived. Some of it he hid on the roof of a glue-factory where the gutter came within reach of the flat top of the washhouse in the back-court. Some of it he put inside an old pair of wellingtons under his bed and stuffed sheets of newspaper on top of it. He was careful never to carry much of it about with him, but he had between four and five hundred pounds he could get at quickly, and he set himself up as a rival to Percy. He liked giving money away. It made him feel big.

Noddy put the twenty pounds into his own hoard, and kept the two ten-shilling notes in his pocket as spending money. He was delighted with them, so delighted that he had no desire to spend them. Two bits of paper were twice as good as one, and he valued Savage's gift of the two half-notes more than he valued Percy's donation of a single pound. The ten-shilling notes were beautiful. He would sit looking at them, marvelling at the curly lines round the heading, Bank of England, and puzzling over the words 'Promise to pay the Bearer on Demand the sum of Ten Shillings', with more curly lines round the last line. What did it mean, *Promise to pay Ten Shillings*, when this bit of russet and dirty-white paper was itself ten shillings? He stared hard at the seated lady on the left with a long pole in her hand and wondered who she was. And beneath her was a long number and beneath the number there were the words *Ten Shillings* in a frame with curly lines all round it. Up at the right there was the same number, and a fancy design with 10 Shillings in the centre. On the back, inside a lot of feathers or dead leaves, it said 10/- twice. So there was no doubt it was ten shillings. Then why promise to pay ten shillings for it? Or what was 'on demand'? It hypnotized him. Probably no one had ever looked so long and so hard and so often at a mere ten shilling note as Noddy did that weekend.

He was still at it when he was back at school on the Monday. He had one of them under the desk when Jasper was at the board trying to teach the division of fractions.

'Three-quarters divided by one-half equals three over four multiplied by two over one,' he jabbered, scribbling with the chalk as he went through it, 'equals six over four equals one and a half'.

He turned to look at his class. They were staring at the blackboard with a glazed look, stunned, stupefied and speechless, all except Noddy. His eyes were equally glazed, but not at the four-line transmutation of three-quarters into one and a half. He was admiring one of his ten-shilling notes.

Silent in his rubber-soled shoes, Jasper prowled over to the faraway boy. He wore rubber soles as an economy measure, for on his salary he couldn't afford two pairs of shoes and a motor-bike as well. He was a poor man. Noddy hadn't heard a word of the gabble at the blackboard, but now he heard the silence and looked up sharply to see what was wrong. He was too late. Jasper pounced.

'Where did you get that?' he breathed in horror, holding the note reverently by the corner while Noddy cowered, fretting the fingers of his empty hands.

'It's no' mines,' he answered swiftly.

'Go and stand in the corner, Mann,' said Jasper. 'Mines is things you go down. Coal mines, copper mines, gold mines. The correct possessive pronoun is mine. I'm sick and tired telling you that. I might as well talk to a brick wall.'

Noddy exasperated him much as Percy had exasperated Miss Elginbrod half a dozen years earlier. He couldn't help picking on Noddy, the boy pulled at him like a magnet. He pushed him into the corner with his face against the wall, and snorted at him 'Hum! Hm! Mann! Some man!'

And then he said, as he had said so often before, for Noddy had an ugly face with a broad flat nose and a scowl like Beethoven's, 'You're no more like a man than a monkey.'

He stood behind the boy, turning the note over and over. It seemed real all right. He was taken by a sudden anger that this unwashed urchin should have ten bob in the middle of the month when he himself hadn't much more.

'There's something fishy about this and I'm going to find out what it is. Where did you get it?'

'Found it,' said Noddy, over his shoulder.

'Where?' Jasper asked, caressing his blue chin between thumb and forefinger.

'Forget,' Noddy said in a half-hearted whisper.

Jasper brought the headmaster into it. Mr Daunders was an experienced man. He had a talent for questioning pupils who were found with more money than they could reasonably be expected to have. The school was full of midgie-rakers, petty thieves, pickpockets, raiders of their mothers' lean purse, breakers of gas-meters, milk-round embezzlers, robbers of weans sent on a shopping errand. What else could you expect in a Glasgow slum where the buildings had been condemned thirty years ago and were still standing as warrens where smalltime criminals proliferated?

'Leave him to me,' he told Jasper. 'I'll get to the bottom of this.'

So Noddy stood on the strip of carpet in front of the headmaster's desk, and the headmaster sat behind the desk and played with a bone paper knife. The offending ten-shilling note flat in front of him, Mr Daunders looked calmly and benignly at the suspect. He saw an undersized boy wearing a ragged grey jersey and torn jeans tucked into a pair of wellingtons, a flattened, frightened dirty face and dark eyes as uncommunicative as the eyes of a wild animal.

'That's far too much money for a wee boy like you to be carrying about,' he began pleasantly. 'Where did you get it?'

'Mamurrer,' Noddy mumbled.

'Your mother gave you it?' Mr Daunders interpreted.

Noddy nodded.

'Why?' said Mr Daunders.

'Go a message,' said Noddy.

'What were you to get?' Mr Daunders asked.

'Forget,' said Noddy.

'I see,' said Mr Daunders. 'And where were you to go for this message?'

'Doh-no,' said Noddy.

'I see,' said Mr Daunders. 'Your mother gave you ten shillings to get something you've forgotten in a shop you don't know. That's not a very good answer, young man. Now just tell me the truth.'

'Muncle gay me it,' Noddy offered.

'Why?' asked Mr Daunders.

'For ma birthday,' said Noddy.

'I see,' said Mr Daunders. He drew open a card-index box at his right hand, flicked to Mann, Nicholas and took out the card. 'And when did your uncle give you this rather generous birthday present?'

'Lass night,' said Noddy.

'I see,' said Mr Daunders. He waved the index card gently. 'And can you tell me why your uncle should give you ten shillings for your birthday last night when your birthday was five months ago?'

Noddy couldn't. He said nothing.

'Did he forget about you for five months?' Mr Daunders asked.

'Yes, sir,' Noddy whispered respectfully.

Mr Daunders sighed.

'No, I don't believe you're telling me the truth yet,' he said sadly. 'Now I'm not accusing you of anything, I'm not saying you stole this money, I'm not saying a thing against you. I just don't believe you're telling me the whole truth. I wouldn't be doing my duty if I didn't make inquiries when a boy is found playing in class with a ten-shilling note he can't explain how he got.'

Noddy clenched his toes inside his wellingtons and said nothing.

'All right,' said Mr Daunders. 'Suppose it was your uncle. Is that your father's brother or your mother's brother?'

'Ma murrer's,' said Noddy. He hadn't seen his father for a couple of years. His mother always visited Barlinnie alone.

'I see,' said Mr Daunders. 'Then what you're saying is that Mr Mann gave you ten shillings for your birthday five months late. Well, better late than never. Is that right?'

Noddy granted the point with another nod.

'You're sure?' Mr Daunders asked. 'Quite sure?'

Noddy nodded.

'But how could he be Mr Mann if he's your mother's brother?' Mr Daunders asked softly.

The soil on Noddy's plain cheeks was irrigated by two parallel streams.

'Ah now, there's no use crying,' said Mr Daunders, a forefinger raised. 'You tell the truth and you'll have no need to cry. Once you tell me the truth you'll have nothing to worry about.'

Noddy thrust one hand into the pocket of his jeans to grope for the other ten-shilling note and draw comfort through his finger tips from the touch of it.

'Come, come,' said Mr Daunders. 'You don't stand before your headmaster with your hand in your pocket. Stand up straight with your hands by your side.'

Then he saw something dart through Noddy's alien eyes, a passing fear, a swift alarm, and the hand seemed unwilling to come out of the pocket. He saw he had missed a move.

'Turn out your pockets,' he said. 'Let me see just what else you're hiding.'

He sighed and tutted over the second ten-shilling note and put it on top of the first.

'And who gave you this one?' he asked wearily.

'Ma murrer,' said Noddy.

'To get messages?' Mr Daunders suggested.

Noddy agreed in his usual way.

'And she gave you the other one too?' Mr Daunders prompted. 'Not your uncle, your mother. Your mother gave you them both?'

Noddy nodded.

'But she'd already given you one ten-shilling note to get messages. Why did she give you two?'

'Case Ah loast wan,' Noddy tried bravely.

'No', said Mr Daunders. 'That won't do, Nicholas. I'm not saying you stole this money. But I don't think you're telling me the truth.'

'Please sir, si truth,' Noddy wept.

The interrogation went on from six minutes past eleven till seventeen minutes past twelve. But Noddy wouldn't say Savage's name, or Percy's, or mention the cellar. He was bound by his oath, and he was more afraid of the consequences of breaking it than of Mr Daunders. If his arms were paralysed and withered and shrivelled and dropped off like the leaves from the trees in autumn he would never be able to play the piano. He might as well be dead as have no arms. Nothing Mr Daunders could do would be as bad as losing his arms. He prayed to El to give him strength and he called out to Percy in the lonely darkness of his soul, and he gave nothing away. Mr Daunders tied him in knots, unravelled them, and tied new ones. Noddy didn't care. It always surprised him how grown-ups dug into a story that wasn't worth listening to. He said he had saved the money, he said he had found it, he said his mother had given him it, he said his uncle had given him it, he said his mother had given him one note and his uncle the other, he said he had saved one and found one, he said a big boy who had left school had given him them to keep for him, but he didn't know the big boy's name, didn't know where he lived, where he worked, or what school he had gone to. He said he had just happened to put his hands in his jeans and found the two notes that morning in class and he had no idea how they got there.

'Two ten-shilling notes, that's one pound,' said Mr Daunders thoughtfully, smoothing the notes on his desk. 'Well, I still think it's a lot of money for a boy like you to be carrying about. Especially when you're not very sure how you come to have so much.'

He stared hard at the ragged dirty urchin and shook his head in defeat. A brief smile jerked at Noddy's frog-like mouth. He was thinking of the daftness of all this fuss about a couple of half-notes when he had hundreds of pounds in fivers and singles stowed away safely to buy a piano when his mother got a new house in the scheme. It would be a rare surprise for her. But he couldn't buy a piano so long as they were living in a single end. He kept his hoard in a waterproof bag inside the cistern in the stairhead lavatory, and his mother thought he was suffering from diarrhoea, he went to the closet so often, but he was only making sure his piano-money was still safe. He loved counting it.

Mr Daunders recognized that the twist in Noddy's enormous mouth was a smile, and he frowned severely.

'There's nothing funny about it, you know,' he said. 'You were crying earlier on. I don't see why you should be smiling now. I'm going to keep this money and I'm going to send for your mother, and I'll get to the bottom of this yet.'

CHAPTER SEVEN

Mr Daunders called in Noddy's mother right away. She was a cleaner in the school, so he had no trouble getting in touch with her. He waited on after four o'clock till she came in for her evening's chores. But it didn't get him anywhere. She stood in his little room, a timid foot and no more inside the door, with her working-overall on and scarf round her head in royal fashion, a big-bosomed, enormous-hipped, thick-ankled woman. That this hulk of womanhood should be the old block of a skelf like Noddy made Mr Daunders think of the mountain that gave birth to a mouse, and as he remembered the phrase he sighed at the destiny that had condemned him to be a headmaster in a small primary school in one of Glasgow's wild-life reservations, a pocket of vandalism, a pool of iniquity. He had a painful stab of longing to have done with backward and delinquent children and be a retired headmaster living his own life, following his own interests. He had an elegant eighteenth century edition of Horace with the mad Christopher Smart's prose translation facing the Latin. He always took it with him when he went on holiday, but somehow he never found time to open it. Now he couldn't even remember where it was that Horace had spoken of the mountain in labour giving birth to a mouse. 'I must read Horace again when I retire,' he thought, even as he was talking severely to Mrs Mann.

Mrs Mann had her own distracting thoughts. According to the book of words only widows were supposed to be employed as cleaners in Corporation schools, and she wasn't technically a widow though she passed for one in so far as she didn't have the support of a husband. A husband in jail for robbery with violence wasn't a resident head of the house. She felt entitled to her job, but she was afraid Mr Daunders was going to tell her she was sacked. When she understood he was talking about her son she felt quite happy and smiled encouragingly to the headmaster. Mr Daunders frowned at her. He knew quite well she was no widow, he knew where her husband was. He had hoped his knowledge might be used as a lever to extract information from her. But she had no information for him. Yet she was the only person who gained from the interview.

She challenged Noddy that night.

'I was hearing you was found wi' more money than you're supposed to have,' she said, slapping his face to begin the discussion on the proper terms. 'Two ten-shilling notes, eh? Now where the hell did you get two ten-shilling notes?'

Noddy said he had found them in a midgie in Ossian Street. There was a bank at the close. The bank must have thrown them out by mistake. They were in an envelope.

'Ha-ha, a likely story!' said Mrs Mann her fingers splayed on her hips. She didn't think of asking for the envelope as Mr Daunders would certainly have done. 'And what did you never think of telling me you found them for if that was how you got them?'

'Ah never goat a chance,' Noddy mumbled, crouched in a corner of the kitchen near the sink, his right hand over his ear. Mrs Mann darted swiftly and smacked his left ear and Noddy changed guard.

'Ye hid nae intentions o' tellin' me, ye little bugger!' she screamed, and then smacked his right ear. Noddy put both hands up.

'Ah hud,' he said. 'Ah've never saw you since Ah fun them. Ah only fun them this moarning.'

'And whit wur ye gaun tae dae wi' them?' said Mrs Mann, pursuing her beloved seventh son as he edged round the kitchen past the dresser and the coal-bunker, along the valance of the recess-bed, up to the fireplace, and behind the ruptured armchair that flanked it.

'Ah wis gaun tae gie ye hauf,' said Noddy, willing to give up one of the bits of paper for the sake of peace.

'Oh, ye wis, wis ye?' said Mrs Mann sceptically. 'Well, come on then! Let's see ye hauf it!'

'Ah canny, he's goat them both,' Noddy wept in vexation.

'Oh, the bastard! So he hus!' cried Mrs Mann, and shook her fists at the whitewashed ceiling above the pulley where her shift and a pair of bloomers were drying, her head thrown back and her bleary eyes staring wildly.

And just as Mr Daunders had waited for her at four o'clock she waited for him at nine o'clock the next morning after she had finished her morning chores. She was humble, garrulous, apologetic, over-explanatory and nervous, but quite firm. Noddy had taken the money from her purse. It was a terrible thing to have a son that would steal from his own mother who had always done the best she could for him, but he was only a boy and he wasn't very bright, he just liked to play with bits of coloured paper, so if she could have her money back, she paused and leered in expectant servility.

Mr Daunders knew when he was beaten. He gave her the two ten-shilling notes, and since she was an honest woman and a good mother she didn't keep them both. She gave one to Noddy.

'There y'are, ma son,' she said tenderly, and threw him across the kitchen in the excess of her affection. 'There's your share like you promised me. And the next time you find anything jist you let me know and don't go causing a lot of bother keeping things tae yersel. Ye've goat tae let yer mammy know. Yer mammy's yer best friend.'

Noddy took the note silently. He didn't know what he wanted to do with it, but it was good to have it in his pocket again.

'Ah ye're a guid wee boy,' his mother grinned, and she rumped his long uncombed hair. Noddy jerked his head away and scowled. Any show of affection distressed him.

He was even more upset to find he was in the bad books of the Brotherhood. The news of his interrogation had spread with the speed of foot and mouth disease, and he was brought on his knees before Percy at the next Friday Night Service. Percy was frightened. First the stranger and now Noddy's two ten-shilling notes. He saw them as two straws that suggested there was a wind rising somewhere, but he didn't know where to look for it.

'I gave you a pound note,' he said severely to Noddy. 'How did you come to be caught with a couple of ten-bob notes? Tell me that.'

'I changed the note you gave me,' Noddy declared, primed in advance by Savage. He tried to rub one of his knees as he was forced to remain on them by Specky and Skinny while the Regent Supreme examined him. It was a most uncomfortable position. He wasn't used to it. Looking at the squalid urchin Percy had an idea. He must get them all to kneel during the Friday Night Service.

'What did you go and get it changed for?' he demanded with the soul-searching stare in his mournful eyes again.

'Because,' said Noddy. 'Let me go, let me up! Ah never told nuthin. Ah swear it, Ah kept the oath. You ask old Daundy. He'll tell you Ah never told him nuthin.'

'What did you change it for if you're saving up?' Percy

persisted. 'You're sure nobody else has been giving you grace?'

'Course Ah'm sure,' Noddy complained, rubbing the other knee ostentatiously. 'Let me up! Ah've got a sore knee. Sure you're the only one with a key. Who else could it be?'

'If I find any of yous fellows coming in here behind my back,' Percy addressed the congregation threateningly, 'I'll burn the whole lot, so I will. Have you no respect for nothing? I made you make a gentlemen's agreement, I taught you about El and how powerful he is if you keep him secret, and now you go flashing ten-bob notes in the school. I don't like it. If there's the least danger of strangers getting a lead into the sanctuary of El we'd be much better to burn the chests and all that's in them. I'm warning yous.'

'Don't be daft,' said Savage, squatting at the right foot of the Regent. 'You're the only wan wi' a key. Whit are ye worrying aboot?'

'All right,' Percy said grudgingly. 'I'll let it go but I'm telling yous I don't like it, I don't like it one little bit, so I don't but.'

Savage smiled, and Percy passed sentence. Noddy was condemned to forfeit payment for four weeks for being caught in possession of the money they had all sworn never to be found with. Noddy wasn't bothered. It was enough for him that he could get up off his knees. He relied on Savage for the month that followed. Savage had promised to give him double his ration if he didn't let Percy find out where the ten-shilling notes had come from.

His mother wasn't bothered either when the other cleaners talked about her son being up before the head-master for stealing money.

'He never stole it, he found it,' she said, choosing to concede at last that she had heard them talking behind her back and under her nose. She shook out a duster as if she were a toreador at a bullfight, her torso swivelling on her enormous hips. 'And I may say for your information if

70

you're interested that my Nicky is a good son to me. Anything he does steal he brings straight home to his maw. He's always been a good boy, I don't care what yous say about him.'

'There's nobody saying anything about him,' said Mrs Phinn, gaunt and chilling.

'Not bloody much,' said Mrs Mann. 'Dae yous think I don't hear ye? Dae yous think I'm bloody-well deaf?'

'I was only saying I wish my Percy could find a couple of ten-shilling notes and give me one of them,' said Mrs Phinn from about three storeys above her.

'Him,' snorted Mrs Mann. 'Your Percy couldna find his way frae here tae there withoot tripping ower his big feet. Him! He couldna gie ye a kind look, he's that bloody sour. Ma wee fella's aye cheery anyway, I'll say that for him. He doesna go aboot wi' a face that wid turn milk.'

'He was never a midgie-raker anyway, my Percy,' said Mrs Phinn proudly. 'He was never a lobby dosser like some weans that never see their faither.'

The vernacular struck home and Mrs Mann could only grunt contemptuously. The janitor was coming along anyway to break it up. She couldn't deny Noddy had been a lobby dosser more than once in his short life. A lobby was the word for the long stairhead landing found in older tenements, and a dosser was a person who slept there. So a lobby dosser was a waif, stray or vagrant who took shelter at night in the common stairway of a tenement and went to sleep in the lobby. Noddy had done it often, playing truant and staying away from home for nights on end. But he was always discovered by some man leaving at five or six in the morning to go on the early shift in Singer's or Beardmore's. Yet he never learnt. He would do it a week after he had promised never to do it again. There wasn't all that much difference between sleeping on the stairhead in a strange close and sleeping under the old coats on top of the boards in the recess-bed in his mother's kitchen.

'Come on, my darlings,' Mr Green bustled them jovially. 'You're not paid for standing there arguing the toss. It's time you did some work. I bet you I've got the biggest blethers in Glasgow for cleaners. So she says to me so I says to her. Yap-yap, morning and night. Come on, get cracking.'

They shuffled off, but he came after them with a hand up, remembering.

'Here, wait a minute! Who's got my key for the cellar? I had it hanging up on its nail in my room, and it's not there now. Do any of you know who took it?'

'We've no occasion to go near the cellar,' said Mrs Phinn, her pail with a shovel in it in one hand and her brush in the other. She was the self-appointed spokeswoman for the cleaners because she was the late janitor's widow, but she was far from being the oldest cleaner, and her assumption of seniority didn't increase her popularity with the other widows. 'Nobody here touched your key.'

'Well, somebody's took it,' Mr Green insisted. 'A key doesn't just go for a walk all by itself.'

'Why should we touch your key?' Mrs Phinn asked him straight, putting down her pail and brush and folding her arms across her flat bosom in a position of rebellion. 'We never need to go down there.'

'Maybe no,' Mr Green granted. 'But I've got to get down there, and soon. I've been trying to get down since I came here. I'll need to get a weekend there and clean that place up. I opened the door once and shut it again quick. I'm keeping that place locked now. I don't want Tom, Dick and Harry wandering in there. I'm fair ashamed of it. It would scunner you. It's a real Paddy's market, I'm no' kidding.'

Mrs Phinn glared at him through her NHS spectacles.

'Aye, it's all very well for you,' Mr Green said jovially to avert a quarrel, 'but your man left that place in some bloody mess, so he did. Christ, it's even got a piano in it! How the hell he ever got a piano down those stairs beats me. And what a stupid place to put a piano anyway!'

'Where else was he to put it?' Mrs Phinn asked indignantly. 'That's where he put everything there was no room for. That's where he was told to put things when Mr Gainsborough was headmaster. That was years before your time, of course.'

'Aye, and before Noah's time too by the look of the place,' Mr Green muttered, rather less jovial. 'Did you ever take a look at it? I bet you you'd find St Mungo's report card down there.'

'St Mungo would never have been at this school,' said Mrs Mann, only half-joking. 'He'd have went to a Catholic school.'

'If you think my husband's to blame for the state of that cellar, I'm quite willing to work on Saturday and tidy it up,' Mrs Phinn declared, standing straight and noble between her pail and her brush that leaned against the door of a classroom.

'Oh, so you're after some overtime, are you,' Mr Green clapped hands, rubbed them, and smiled. 'I couldn't put you through for overtime. The Office would never wear it.'

'Not for overtime, for my husband's sake,' Mrs Phinn answered, and drew surplus mucus up her nose in the way that always annoyed Percy. 'If you think you can run him down. He was a janitor before you were born.'

'I'm not running anybody down,' Mr Green soothed her. 'I'm only passing the remark that the cellar's in a bloody mess. Many thanks for your kind offer of course. Nevertheless, notwithstanding, I'd better see to it myself. The trouble is the key's lost.'

'I know all about that piano,' Mrs Phinn said aggrievedly. 'My man told me all about it. He filled in a white requisition to have it uplifted and he was still waiting for them to come when he went and died.'

'Oh, well, ye canna blame him for that,' Mr Green said kindly.

'Maybe wan o' the boys has took it,' Mrs Mann suggested. 'Ye know whit boys is like.'

'Oh, I know,' said Mr Green, nodding his head and tutting. 'They found a kid here the other day with forty-seven keys in his pocket. They pick them up and steal them and borrow them and get another one cut and then they try them on the shop doors and up closes where they think there's nobody in. Oh, ye canna be up to them!'

'Well, I hope you find your key,' said Mrs Phinn, stooping to her pail of sawdust. 'But we can't stand talking to you all night. Some of us has got work to do.'

Mr Green found the missing key back on its nail in his cubbyhole two days later. He never found out that Savage had pinched it and had a duplicate cut in Barrowland quick.

'I'm fly, you see,' Savage boasted to Specky and Noddy. 'I didn't steal that key. I just took a lend o' it and put it back before wee Greeny had time to miss it. You see the idea is you've got to make sure you're not suspicious.'

'So you've a key to get in by Tulip Place and you've a key to get in through the school,' Specky nodded admiration.

'You're going to cause a lot of trouble,' Skinny muttered sadly. 'Percy'll find out sooner or later.'

'It was for Percy's sake I done it,' Savage grinned. 'I think he dreams mair nor he sees. But maybe he's right about somebody watchin the door round the corner. So I can get at the money—'

'You're not to say money!' Skinny cried, anguished.

'Well, I can find the road to El through the basement then,' Savage amended unctuously. 'Is that better?'

'And how do you get past the janny's house?' Specky asked. He was offended that an ape like Savage had managed to do more than an intellectual like himself.

'I put my sannies on,' said Savage. 'I know when wee Greeny and his wife are watching the telly, and I just creep across the playground. It's as safe as the Bank.'

'How much have you taken?' Specky asked bluntly.

'Enough,' Savage laughed at him. 'Do ye want to come in? Percy's daft. Ye canna leave it all to him, can ye? I've got enough put away for life.'

'Well, don't you ever boast to Frank Garson or he'll shop you to Percy right away,' warned Specky. 'I think he's suspicious already.'

Mr Green wasn't suspicious.

74

'Just one of those things,' he said to his wife when the key turned up. He never made mysteries out of the inexplicable, he never brooded over how, why and wherefore. He simply put aside every anomaly in daily life as 'just one of those things', and went on living his busy life. So far as he thought about the return of the missing key at all he supposed one of the cleaners had taken it in mistake for another, forgotten about it, and put it back in its place rather than own up after he had asked questions about it.

He went down to the cellar alone on the Sunday afternoon, not meaning to do any work, just to estimate how much work would be needed to put the place in order and get rid of the lumber – once he was sure what was lumber and what wasn't. As on his previous visits, a glance was enough to depress him. He went sadly up the narrow steps, shaking his head and far from saying a prayer for the repose of the soul of the late Mr Phinn.

'What a janitor!' he muttered as he locked the door. He felt he had an enormous cupboard there, with countless skeletons. 'It must have been worrying about that place killed him.'

He was quite unwilling to tackle the job of tidying the cellar himself in spite of what he had said to Mrs Phinn. He took her at her word and got her to come in the next Saturday afternoon and work for nothing. To help her, he drafted in another cleaner, Mrs Quick, promising her a few bob out of his own pocket. Mrs Mann heard of the job and offered her services too for a mere tip. Mr Green didn't mind. He knew Mrs Mann was just being nosey and hoping to come by pickings, but he couldn't see what pickings there could be in a cellar full of school rubbish. He stood in at the start of what he called jocularly Operation Underground, gave the three cleaners a general idea of what he wanted done, and when they were started he stealthily slipped upstairs and went out for a pint.

The cleaners were good workers. By shifting the position of the various items, putting like with like, marshalling everything along the walls and sweeping and mopping a central area they created an illusion of tidiness. The cellar certainly looked different when they were finished, and to that extent they had made an improvement in it. Mrs Mann found the three tea-chests hidden behind a rank of broken desks along the darkest wall where the roof of the cellar descended to meet the rising floor halfway under the playground, and rummaged in the first of them. Maybe there was something would never be missed.

'Nosey!' cried Mrs Phinn, scowling from the centre of the cellar, and drawing the back of her rough hand across her sweating brow. She had a sudden jab of pain when she saw Mrs Mann kneeling over the chest. It reminded her of the way she had found her husband, sprawled just like that, stone cold dead over the very same chest.

'How are we to know what's rubbish and what's not if we don't look?' Mrs Mann asked hoity-toitily over her shoulder. 'That's what wee Greeny's paying us for. He wants to know what he can throw out and what he can't. You've got to be nosey to do the job right.'

She plunged into the crate again and surfaced with the fairy wand. She flourished it towards Mrs Phinn and in the voice of a pantomime fairy she chanted. 'And now I banish the wicked witch! Begone, bugger off, you ugly old bitch!'

'Ach, that's the school concert stuff,' Mrs Quick cried with a wave of her broom.

Mrs Phinn's scowl narrowed to a glare. It was the sorrow of her life that she had been the belle of the district between seventeen and nineteen, lost her good looks and her figure, and finished up, she well knew, an ugly old bitch. The worries of marriage, the strain of making ends meet and coping with a husband who kept bad company and drank too much, had ploughed her youth's fair field with furrows of bitterness.

'It's an awful pity they stopped doing a concert every year,' said Mrs Quick. 'I used to enjoy them. They used to do some rare pantomimes and a kind of variety show. And they were good for the weans and a'. It learned them good to speak right.'

Mrs Mann put the wand across one of the broken desks and dived into another tea-chest, her broad bottom level with the edge of the chest as she delved deeper, her head and torso inside. She came up again and turned round with a top hat in her hand.

'Oh, I remember that turn!' Mrs Quick squealed in delight. 'There was wan o' the girls came on dressed like a man and she wore that tile hat. Oh, she was a rare wee dancer!'

Mrs Mann crowned herself with the top hat, picked up the fairy wand again as a walking stick and swayed to the swept centre of the stone floor singing in a broad Glasgow voice.

> *'I'm Burrlington Berrtie,*
> *I rrise at ten therrty,*
> *An' go furr a strroll in the Parrk!'*

She did a little jig with an ease and lightness surprising in a woman of her colossal bulk, but she was used to it. She performed those steps every year when she marched behind the flute band in the Orange Walk on the Twelfth of July.

'You're going back some!' Mrs Phinn commented coldly.

'I used to hear ma maw sing that song,' Mrs Mann explained amiably. 'She'd be about your age.'

'Ach, yer granny's mutch!' Mrs Phinn retorted contemptuously. 'You stand there and do a song and dance act but it's me that's doing all the work and getting nothing for it and you're doing nothing and getting paid for it. It's no' fair.'

Encouraged by Mrs Mann's entertainment Mrs Quick delved into the third of the chests and dragged out a brocade jacket.

'That's what the Baron wore the year they did Cinderella,' she screeched, and tried it on.

'Baron Figtree!' Mrs Mann howled, clapped her hands, took a front-stage pose and declaimed a couplet from an old Glasgow pantomime.

> *'Tomorrow's my grandmother's wedding day.*
> *Ten thousand pounds will I give away.'*

'Hooray, hooray, hooray!' Mrs Quick took the cue, with a triple change of voice to suggest the discordant applause of the lads and lasses of the village. Mrs Mann bowed and went on.

> *'On second thought I think it best*
> *To stow it away in the old oak chest.'*

'Boo, boo, boo!' Mrs Quick responded as before.

'When yous two has stopped acting the goat,' Mrs Phinn cut in with clearly enunciated superiority.

Her two helpers leaned over the tea-chests, laughing as only fat women can. That Mrs Phinn had no joy in their turn increased theirs. Mrs Quick wiped her eyes with her duster.

'Well, come on, Jessie,' she wheezed. 'We can tell him this is a' the old concert costumes and he can burn it or dae whit he likes wi' it.'

'Shove them up against the wa', Maggie,' said Mrs Mann. 'The three o' them. Then we can tell him they're a' the gither.'

Mrs Mann kept the top hat. If she couldn't pawn it Noddy might be able to use it when he dressed up for Hallowe'en. It would maybe earn him a few extra coppers round the doors or on the street. She was always thinking about money.

'We could tell some o' the weans there's a lot of good stuff down here for when it's Hallowe'en.'

'Aye, they could get some rare fancy clobber here,' Mrs Quick agreed, thrusting the top layers of chests down hard to make them look tidy.

'I don't suppose it matters there's no false-faces,' Mrs Phinn muttered. 'Your Nicky wouldny need one.'

'Ho, ho,' Mrs Mann replied, pushing the third of the chests alongside its mates. 'Very clever, I must say.'

CHAPTER EIGHT

Percy was the first to see the cellar had been entered. He came down by the chute on Sunday night, making his usual visit to what had become a sanctuary to him, and stopped at once when he reached the floor. He thought he was going to faint. For the first time in his life he understood what it meant to get a shock. Something seemed to have hit him in the midriff, his heart went vaulting and then tumbled, his legs were paralysed, his head was a clamour of alarm bells, his eyes were in a mist one moment and as sharp as an eagle's the next, his palate was parched and his tongue was stuck to it, his brow felt chilled, and he nearly wet himself.

When he recovered from the seizure he galloped over to the chests, almost tripping himself on his splay feet in his excitement. His torso was so far ahead of his legs that he seemed to mean to get there by bodily extension rather than by running. He saw the concert props and costumes weren't quite as they had been left. Some that had been in different chests were now in the same chest, some that had been underneath were now on top. He leaned over the first chest, pulled out skirts, hats, jackets, trousers, cardboard capstans and festoons of coloured paper, and delved to the bottom. The money was still there. And so with the other chests. Whoever had been in the cellar and swept it out and moved the chests hadn't disturbed more than the top layers. The transistor, the tape-recorder and record-player, the TV and the uke and the guitar were still safe against the farthest and darkest wall of the cellar, the rats' wall, behind a façade of planks, pails and the barrel of washing-soda. So much for the thoroughness of the cleaners' cleaning. He knelt beside one of the chests with his hands clasped and said a sincere prayer of thanks.

'Oh, blessed El, I thank thee for not allowing thyself to

fall into the hands of the ungodly,' he panted, his mouth against his finger-tips.

He thought of moving the money, but he didn't know where else he could put it. If it had survived one attack in the cellar it could survive another. The cellar still seemed the safest place for it, and the proper place too, since it had been found in the cellar. He was unwilling to find a new site for what had always been safe in the place where it was discovered. The cellar seemed its natural and even sacred place because that was where El had chosen to reveal himself. Even the distribution amongst three chests had a mystical meaning to him. He couldn't bear to tamper with fortune by shifting anything.

He called an extraordinary assembly at once, held a special service, and declared an extra dividend in thanksgiving for the safety of El. The Brotherhood didn't mind the special service, they liked singing together, and they took the extra share-out gladly enough. But looking down from his throne Percy noticed signs of a strange uninterest here and there, an air of forced swallowing. There came to him suddenly the memory that he had helped the woman in charge of the dinner-school once when he was a boy, and she had given him a double helping of ice-cream after the diners were all gone. He took it eagerly. It was three or four times as large as the largest ice he had ever had before. Then she gave him a second plateful, just to be nice to him, and he got through it only because it was impossible to refuse ice-cream. But he was sick afterwards, and it made him think less of ice-cream in the future.

'It was only the cleaners, ye know,' Savage explained wisely after the service. 'The way you talk you'd think it was evil spirits had raided the place.'

'Maybe you don't believe it, but the world's full of evil spirits,' said Percy.

'Oh aye, I believe that,' said Savage with flippant solemnity.

'I know it was the cleaners was in,' Percy tried again. 'I'm perfectly well aware of that, but the point is what made them come down here. Nobody's ever been down here before. If that wasn't the promptings of evil spirits, what was it? Go on, you tell me! And what's more it's a miracle they didn't find anything. That shows we're being looked after. You've got to believe in destiny, ye know. Kismet. Kay Sarah, Sarah.'

'It was wee Noddy was telling me his maw was in here Saturday afternoon,' Savage answered conversationally, refusing to ask who Sarah was. He knew Percy was just dying to explain it to him. 'He knew by the Saturday night everything was okay. His old girl never mentioned a thing. Your maw was down as well. Did she no' tell ye? Jees, that would have had ye worried stiff if she'd said to ye, I'm going down the cellar to clean it out!'

Percy snubbed him silently. He hadn't known his mother was in the cellar on Saturday. He had missed her in the afternoon, but he hadn't asked where she had been and she didn't tell him. It made his head ache to think of the danger they had been in. His headaches were becoming a daily plague, and he blamed them on the strain he was under, being responsible for the safety of thousands of pounds and the welfare of a horde of ungrateful boys. And so it would go on till something happened. Something was bound to happen. But he couldn't imagine what it was. He lived in fear of a knock at the door. Every time he passed a policeman he felt nervous. He dreamt nearly every night of the stranger who had accosted him in Tulip Place, and waited patiently for his bad dreams to come true. The stranger must reappear. He knew there was no escape from him. He felt all alone and powerless. It came back to him that he had wanted to have a lot of money so that he could get peace. And now he had less peace than ever. He had the money, but his mind wasn't free to write poetry. But would Shelley have written any poetry if he had to look after a street-gang? He made up his mind to start tomorrow and organize his life better, so as to find time and peace to begin writing a poem. But it was always a case of starting tomorrow. He groaned, sitting on Miss Elginbrod's chair, and put his head between his hands, his elbows on his knees.

'Headache?' piped Savage brightly in a commercial TV voice. 'Be good to yourself! Take a Scrunchy-Lunchy. Six good points for sixpence. Makes you one shade lighter. Scrunchy-Lunchy's good for weans, puts an end to aches and pains. Take a Scrunchy-Lunchy tonight and tomorrow you'll—'

'Oh, shut up, you!' Percy snarled at him, turning on his Chief Claviger, taking his hands away to reveal a frustrated face with big bewildered eyes. He hated vulgarity. It added to his distress that he was coming to hate Savage, yet once he had liked him. He had meant to polish a rough diamond, and now he hated the look of it.

Savage was delighted. He had got Percy really annoyed. 'Aw, keep the heid,' he said amiably, and went away.

Drunk with power at having got the better of Percy he caught up on the other members of the Brotherhood at the corner of Tulip Place and entertained them with an imitation of Frank Garson. He couldn't stand Frank Garson, and he couldn't leave him alone. He had always to be making a fool of him because he kept his face clean and spoke politely. His star turn was to put on a West-end voice and repeat something Garson had said. The incongruity of chaste correct speech coming from Savage's loose mouth gave the Brotherhood an uneasy amusement and they laughed guiltily when he imitated a girlish walk to go with his imitation of Garson's girlish voice.

'It was Ai who found the money, but Ai don't want any share, ow now, thenk you. 'Sa metter of fect, Ai think Ai ought to inform the polis.'

He picked up a phone from mid-air, dialled a number in the same place, and squeaked, writhing like a striptease dancer, 'Ello, ello, Sat Whitehall 1212? Ken Ai hev a wurrd with the Chief Constable, pulease? Ello, ello, ello! Statchoo, Chief Ai jist want to report there's an awful lot of boys here has an awful lot of money. Kin Ai claim a reward for telling you?'

'Ach, wheesht,' said Specky, past being amused. 'You'll

make jokes about money once too often. Somebody'll hear you.'

'You know Percy's rule,' Skinny accused him. 'And it's a wise rule too. We promised never to mention money outside.'

'I'm fed up wi' him and his great god El,' Savage retorted lightly. 'Money's money the world over, and ye might as well admit it. Kidding yerself it's something mysterious and supernatural, the way Percy talks, it's daft. Where's wee Garson? I want to see him. Did ye notice he's still no' taking any money?'

They ambled on together, a little gang of them, till they caught up with Frank Garson crossing the waste land between the Steamie and the back of Bethel Street, a desolation of hard earth and dockens.

'Oi, Garsie!' shouted Savage, a domineering note in his voice.

Garson turned obediently and waited. He was always polite, even to people who were rude to him. Savage came close up and flipped his finger tips against the waiting boy's nose.

'When are you gaun tae start taking yer share o' the lolly?' he whispered, smiling maliciously.

It vexed him, it provoked him deeply and sharply, that Garson stuck to his position that they ought to report the finding of the money and wouldn't take any part of it. Garson knew he would never go to the police on his own, especially when they had the money so long, but Savage didn't know that. He was afraid Garson would turn informer and he wanted to incriminate him by forcing money on him. Being a reasonably intelligent youngster, Garson saw what Savage was up to and he had the wit to see that taking a little would make him just as guilty as taking a lot. He determined from the beginning to take nothing and he was nowhere near yielding now. He would keep his hands clean against the day of reckoning that would certainly come. But he went to the Friday Night Service every week because he enjoyed the strangeness of it in the candlelight.

Percy's sermons and the hymn singing satisfied a longing for communion with his mates. He was lonely, and he needed the Brotherhood, he was still so young.

'Are ye feart somebody catches ye wi' a pound note in yer pocket?' Savage persisted against the silence facing him.

'I just don't want any money,' Garson answered simply. 'That's all. I think you're all making a terrible mistake. And you'll be sorry one day. You'll see.'

'Then you shouldn't be coming to the cellar at all,' Savage argued, pushing him away. 'You've no right to be coming to Percy's Friday Night Services. That's only for folk that believe in El, like Percy says, it's no' for heathens like you that believe in nothing.'

He turned and grinned to the gang that had followed him in pursuit of Garson, amused at his use of Percy's language and wanting them to be amused too. They watched with dull faces.

'I go to them because I want to,' Garson said boldly. 'I don't have to defend myself to you. I've a right to go. It was I who found the money.'

'I tellt ye, I tellt ye!' Savage crowed triumphantly to the gang. 'Oh boy, oh boy! It was Ai who! Oh brush my shoes, Cherlie! My maw's a duchess!'

He flicked a finger tip against the tip of Garson's nose and asked abruptly, 'How is yer maw noo? Dyever see her?'

The flick in the nose angered Garson. It was surprisingly painful. It made his eyes water. In an instinctive response he hit out at Savage and missed him. Savage cackled and danced round him.

'Haw, haw! Ye couldna hit a coo on the erse wi' a banjo!'

Garson lunged again and missed again.

'Haw, haw, ye hivna got a maw!' Savage chanted the rude rhyme, and sang on malevolently, 'Yer maw ran awa' wi' a darkie.'

'She didn't!' Garson screamed in a frenzy. Yet it was all he had ever heard said, and his denial was an act of faith in the ultimate goodness of the universe. If he accepted com-

84

mon gossip as the truth then the world was bad, but the world couldn't be bad. It was good, Percy was good. His father was good. School was good. The stories he read were good. He tried to grapple with Savage, to catch him and choke him, but he was far too slow, and he was blinded with tears of anguish. Then as he blundered and lurched this way and that way, Savage stood stock still and faced up to him.

'Come on and I'll fight you then,' he said, suddenly grim and blood-thirsty.

The Brotherhood formed a ring with a rapid manoeuvre worthy of well-trained troopers, and the surplus members climbed on to the top of the pre-nuclear-age air-raid shelters to watch the fight from there and cheer the winner from a ringside seat.

Garson blinked, trying to see his enemy clearly through tears that reflected a cruel world. He had a brief intuition that the people were evil after all, and if that was how it was there was no use fighting. He was beaten before he started. He was no fighter anyway. He was smaller, slighter, far less of a brawler by build and temperament than Savage. But he had to fight even though it was useless. He would die honourably. He shaped up clumsily, nervously, and while he was still making up his mind whether to lead with the left hand or the right Savage punched him right on the nose with one hand and then bang on the eye with the other.

Garson yelped and wept, and Savage hit him in the stomach. He put his hands there to console the shock and Savage smacked him on the ear. In a few seconds he was a quivering helpless morsel of inadequate boyhood. Blood came down his nose over his lips and he was squeamish at the salty taste of it, the water brimming over his eyes kept him from seeing right, and the bells ringing in his ear made him lose all sense of balance and direction. He stumbled and flailed. Still he wouldn't give in. He wouldn't turn and run. He didn't know where to run to. He kept on trying to fight, but he had no idea of fighting. Savage was radiant

85

with the lust of punishment. He had no mercy. He was a wily battering ram, and Garson was the young lamb bleating at the slaughter.

Skinny filtered silently through the rowdy mob as soon as he saw it was a case of murder, and ran for Percy. He found him with his big feet in Tulip Place and his head in the clouds. He was thinking about the stranger. He was always thinking about the stranger. But now he was beginning to feel safe again, it was so long since he had seen him. He was rather proud of his plan for making sure nobody entered or left the cellar if there was anyone odd hanging about the corner: one of the Brotherhood stayed outside at every service and if he saw any stranger he was to play in Tulip Place and keep kicking a ball against the cellar door as if he was practising shooting and collecting rebounds. That was the warning. A simple signal that no stranger could recognize for what it was, Percy was sure. So far there had been no need for the sentry to kick a ball against the door. Perhaps the stranger had gone away for good. Perhaps he was in jail. He looked a real jail-type. Whatever he was he didn't seem to be a danger any longer.

Last to leave the cellar, the dreaming lord of uncounted wealth, Percy paid off the sentry and ambled down Tulip Place in grim meditation, welcoming the headache it gave him as the price he had to pay for being a thinker. It was all very well looking after a crowd of ungrateful schoolboys, but it was time he did something for himself too. He had his career to think of. All this time gone and he hadn't even got around to finishing that Ode to Speed he had started.

'Savage is killing Garson!' Skinny yelled, grabbing the Regent by one gaunt wrist and shaking it madly.

'Whit are ye talking aboot noo?' Percy grumbled crossly. He left the island in the Mediterranean where he had a patio or hacienda or something like that, he wasn't sure which, but he had in mind a big house with a verandah, and came unwillingly back to Tulip Place.

'He's fighting him and Garson canny fight,' Skinny explained in a hurry. 'It's blue murder so it is. Come on and stop it, Percy! Please! Afore he kills him. Ye ought to see the state he's in, it's terrible!'

'Whit way could you no' stop it?' Percy demanded, forced to trot as Skinny, still clutching his wrist, turned and raced across the street, through a close, across the back-court, and over to the waste land beside the Steamie. 'Or Specky? Fat lot o' use there was making yous somebody. You never use the authority I gave you. How would it be if I just let yous all do whit ye like? Tell me that.'

He grumbled all the way, but Skinny said nothing. He let Percy grumble. He saw no point answering such daft questions. How could he ever stop Savage hitting anybody he wanted to hit? There were things you just had to give in to and put up with, like the brute force of Savage. He had taken a big enough risk running away to fetch Percy. He could only hope that in the excitement nobody would notice it was he who brought Percy along and that he would be safe from the later vengeance of Savage for spoiling him of his prey.

The Brotherhood opened to let Percy get into the ring and he splay-footed indignantly over to Savage, who was kicking Garson in the ribs as the boy cowered on the ground with his head in his arms and his shoulders shaking with sobs. Percy hit Savage an open-handed smack across the face, so hard that the sound was clearly heard by the spectators on top of the air-raid shelters, and they gasped an 'Oo-oo-oo!' of mingled delight and alarm at the violence of the blow.

'You chuck that!' Percy shouted angrily. 'Or I'll give you a kicking, so I will. You're nothing but a big bully. You think you can settle everything by force. Whatever you're fighting about fighting proves nothing. I've tellt ye that before. Can ye no' take a telling?'

He glared down at Savage, heaving with temper, and Savage rubbed his cheek and grinned up at him amiably. He wasn't bothered. His lust was satisfied. A smack on the face was a small price to pay for leaving Garson a bloody weeping humiliated victim on the ground. His father had hit him harder often for nothing.

Percy shook him at the throat, almost lifting him off the ground, and Savage wriggled and wrenched himself away.

'It was nothing,' he said innocently. 'Keep the heid, Percy. The wee fella wanted to have a square go so I gave him wan and he couldny take it, that was a'. You don't need to start shouting the odds aboot it.'

Garson got on his knees, then on his feet, and brushed himself with trembling hands, little soft white hands that couldn't have punched a bus-ticket. His lower lip was going as if he had a permanent stammer and he was still crying.

Percy wanted to comfort him, to stand up for him, to avenge him. His brain was in a mist of pity. But he had sworn never to have favourites in the Brotherhood because that would only cause strife and jealousy. He swallowed his loving anguish for the unfriended boy till the bitterness of it made him grue. Then he spoke out harshly, shaking Garson as he had shaken Savage.

'What do you want to go starting fights for? You know damn fine you're no' a match for Sheuchie Savage, ye wee fool!'

Garson suffered the shaking patiently as long as it lasted, and the moment he was released he turned and went away. The mob opened an alley for him and let him pass along without a whisper of sympathy or a hand raised to console him with a pat on the back, and he went off shaking his head as if Percy's large hand was still at his collar.

'Ye're a horde of ruffians!' Percy cried in exasperation, feeling he had let Garson down but not knowing what else he could have done.

'Yous that was watching and made no attempt to stop it, yous are just as bad as Savage, only worse. We've got all this – all this—'

He paused and the Adam's apple in his scraggy neck moved up and down, but it was a crisis to him and he had to say it.

'All this money. Aye, all this money. Yous know damn

well what I mean. We've got all this money and yous canny live in peace. I give yous up! Come on, get away home all of yous! Scram! Come on, run, run, run! Every one of yous, beat it!'

Normally the false plural slipped from him only now and again. He had learned it was wrong, and he was trying hard to stop using it. But he was too angry to think of his grammar.

He waved his gang away with open hands like a farmer's wife shooing hens, and those on the ground dispersed slowly, resenting his command to run, and those on the roof of the air-raid shelters jumped down and mixed guiltily with their brethren. In a few moments Percy was all alone in the waste land.

'Hate!' he muttered unhappily. 'It's only brought hate. Those two hate each other. It could have made them so happy if they would only be reasonable. I should have made them make it up before wee Frankie went away. I should have made them shake hands and be friends. It's an awful job, making yourself responsible for folks that hasn't been brought up to what's right.'

CHAPTER NINE

Mr Garson was a lonely man, a dour man. He wasn't given to complaining and he suffered many daily injustices rather than make a fuss, but when he came home from the garage that evening and saw his son's black eye and puffed lips he was just a little bit angry. He was willing to take it as natural that boys should fight now and again, but this hadn't been a fight, it looked more like assault and battery. He wanted to know what had happened, but he couldn't get anything out of the boy, so he shook him by the shoulder in an impatient attempt to make him speak. The boy winced and yelped.

'Take your shirt off,' said Mr Garson sharply. He hadn't grasped him all that roughly, there was no need for such a cry of pain unless the damage was as great elsewhere as it was on the face. He suspected it was, and he wanted to make sure.

Garson stripped grudgingly to the waist, embarrassed to be half-naked in the kitchen under the glowering eye of his unfriendly father. His shoulders were bruised, and his flanks were black and blue where Savage had kicked him.

'You tell me who did that to you or I'll give you worse,' said Mr Garson, quite cold.

The boy would have told him gladly if he had been thawed by a warm sympathy, he would have enjoyed weeping out the name if he had been consoled and pitied, but the cold threat froze him.

'I'm warning you,' said Mr Garson with a frightening sincerity, 'You'd better tell me.'

The boy had a brief fantasy of his father fighting Savage's father to avenge the family honour, but he knew that was absurd. His father was too proud even to speak to Savage's father, far less fight him in the back-court or the waste land. Nor would he rush out to look for Savage and smack his ear. That was just as absurd. He just wanted to know for the sake of knowing. All right then, why shouldn't he tell? He kept his silence for a little longer till he didn't feel quite so frozen inside and then he told.

Mr Garson took time off from the garage on Monday morning and went to the school. He didn't know what he wanted exactly, he certainly didn't want vengeance, but he did want to make a protest and get some kind of assurance it wouldn't happen again. He thought he was likelier to get that from the headmaster than from the parents. Mr Daunders promised to look into it, he offered to have Savage brought in right away and invited Mr Garson to remain and see the boy for himself. Mr Garson said he would rather not.

'So long as you promise me to make sure he gets a lesson, I'll leave it to you,' he said respectfully. He was only a motor-mechanic, and he looked up to Mr Daunders as an educated man.

'I'll give him a lesson all right,' Mr Daunders promised cordially. 'We could do with more pupils like your boy, always clean and smart and industrious, but you see every school has its Savages and that's what makes our job so difficult. It's one long struggle against the jungle here.'

They parted at the door of the headmaster's room, both talking at once in polite expression of mutual trust.

'I'll leave him to you,' said Mr Garson.

'You can safely leave him to me,' said Mr Daunders. 'I wish we had more decent parents like you, Mr Garson.'

He sent for Savage at once and lectured him on the immorality of bullying. For all his confident promises to Mr Garson he wasn't sure of the best way to handle it. He was a good man, a reasonable man, unwilling to damn any boy till he had tried hard to save him. He saw little sense telling Savage it was wrong to think that the use of superior physical force was a good thing, and then going on to give him a lathering with a Lochgelly. It was the use of force he had to discredit. He spoke sternly but reasonably. He tried to make Savage see the dangers of living by jungle law. Savage slouched insolently, his black leather jerkin, with the zip unfastened, bulging out in front of his broad chest. He was a big boy, but Mr Daunders was a man. He looked down on him.

'I've told you before not to wear that belt,' he said severely, 'Take it off. You don't need it.'

Savage took off an Army webbing belt and rolled it in his hand. Many a fight he had won with it.

'Where did you get that jacket, by the way?' Mr Daunders asked curiously. He knew quality when he saw it, and he knew that Savage's father could never afford the price of it. 'I haven't seen you wearing it before.'

'My Granny bought me it,' said Savage.

'For your birthday?' Mr Daunders asked, a vague memory of something he had heard before putting an ironic edge on his question.

''Sright,' Savage nodded willingly, leering up as Mr Daunders looked down. He understood too late what the headmaster was staring at. The bulge of the jacket exposed the lining.

'And what's that you've got in there?' Mr Daunders asked gently, simply gesturing to the lining of the jacket. He was too careful ever to touch a boy's clothing.

Savage's hand flashed to the four pound notes he had pinned inside the jacket that morning.

'Let me see it,' said Mr Daunders.

Savage knew when he was caught. He unpinned the notes and handed them over. He wasn't bothered. He had plenty more.

Mr Daunders scowled at the notes. He didn't like it at all.

'What are you doing with these pinned in your jacket?' he cried in bewilderment. It was always the same. One inquiry always led into another you hadn't expected. You started to question a boy who had simply played truant and before you had finished finding out where he went, you were on the track of a series of thefts from shops and lorries.

'That's where Maverick keeps his money,' Savage stalled.

Mr Daunders wouldn't admit to a scruffy schoolboy that he too followed the adventures of Maverick.

'Whose class is he in?' he asked judicially.

'He's no' in a class, he's on the telly,' Savage explained.

'That hardly tells me what you're doing with four pound notes pinned inside a very expensive leather jacket, does it?' Mr Daunders murmured.

Savage said nothing.

'Where did you get this money?' Mr Daunders asked wheedlingly. 'Come on, you'll save a lot of time, and save yourself a lot of trouble if you tell me the truth. Where did you get it?'

'Wee Noddy gave it to me to keep for him,' Savage answered. He was quick in his own way. He knew it was safe to mention Noddy, because Noddy wouldn't give anything away. He couldn't, because he couldn't speak. To tell about the cellar was far beyond Noddy's powers of speech.

'Who?' said Mr. Daunders, just as unwilling to admit he knew nicknames as to admit he knew Maverick.

'Nicky Mann,' said Savage, 'in Jasper's class.'

'In whose class?' Mr Daunders asked gently. He knew quite well who Jasper was. He had often commented on the amazing knack schoolboys had for giving a teacher a nickname. Jasper was an admirable name for the blue-jowled, villainous-looking young man with the lock of jet-black hair always falling over his right eye.

'Mr Whiffen's,' said Savage. 'Nicky Mann in Mr Whiffen's class.'

'Oh no!' Mr Daunders groaned, his compulsive act of judicial ignorance over. He had to face it.

'I'm keeping this money,' he said. 'Send Mann to me.'

He knew he had blundered the moment Savage crossed the door. He should have kept Savage incommunicado and had someone else fetch Noddy. But he was tired. Tired of evasive, deceitful, dirty-faced schoolboys. He had another spasm of longing for his retirement and his Horace.

Noddy arrived, briefly but efficiently warned by Savage, and Mr Daunders knew he was beaten before he started.

'I never,' said Noddy

'But he says you gave him it,' said Mr Daunders.

'I never,' said Noddy.

'Where did you get it?' asked Mr Daunders.

'I never,' said Noddy.

'Are you saying Savage is telling lies then?' Mr Daunders asked.

'I never,' said Noddy.

'Well, where do you think Savage got it?' Mr Daunders asked.

'I never,' said Noddy.

'You're not answering my question.' Mr Daunders said. 'Just listen to me. Now—'

'I never,' said Noddy.

Mr Daunders gave in. He had to admit it was impossible

to get a statement from a boy who was inarticulate, but that was only what Savage had seen before him.

He kept the four pound notes, though he wasn't happy about it. He insisted on seeing Savage's parents, but it was no use. They never answered his letter inviting them to call, for Savage made sure he got his hands on it first. The loss of the money didn't bother him, he had plenty more. He was more concerned to keep his father out of it.

Mrs Mann was no help either. Noddy told her no more than he told Mr Daunders, and she was too cautious to claim the money. She had a nose. So had Mr Daunders.

'It smells very fishy to me,' he told his chief assistant, a superior person from a Border family with the double-barrelled name of Baillie-Hunter. 'There seems to be a lot of money floating round this school just now. Miss Nairn told me she found McGillicuddy with a pound note inside his reader. He was apparently using it as a bookmark.'

'He always reminds me of those odd mountains in Ireland,' said Mr Baillie-Hunter, sniffing languidly. 'McGillicuddy's Reeks.'

'He does smell a little,' Mr Daunders conceded. 'You see, they never wash all over, and they sleep in their shirt, these boys.'

'And McCutcheon had money last week,' said Mr Baillie-Hunter.

'Yes, Mr Wiffen caught him passing a ten-shilling note to Morrison when they were supposed to be doing their sums,' said Mr Daunders. 'And Miss McIvory found out Somerled was paying McIntosh and Crombie five bob a week each to do his homework for him. One of them did his arithmetic and the other did his grammar. There he was, getting his homework right every time and couldn't get a thing right in class. The deceit was as gross as a mountain, open, palpable. They've no craft, these boys. His mother was up to see me only yesterday. Quite cross because I hadn't approved him for a full senior secondary course. She wanted to argue he was a clever boy. Always got his homework right. She damn soon changed her tune when I showed her his dictation book. Forty, fifty and sixty errors in dictations of less than a hundred words.'

'Oh, we could never send him to a senior secondary school,' said Mr Baillie-Hunter, appalled. 'Why, he doesn't even know his tables.'

'Ah, they're a great lot!' Mr Daunders sighed. 'I don't know what I did to be sent here as headmaster in my declining years. I might as well be in the CID, the things I've got to investigate. And what am I to do about this four pound? It isn't mine, and I'm damn sure it isn't Savage's. Do you think they could be selling what they steal? There's a sort of gang there, you know, Savage – he's the ringleader, I'm sure – and Noddy and Cuddy and Cutchy and Somerled. Wherever you find trouble in this school you find they're mixed up in it.'

'What about Tosh and Crumbs?' Mr Baillie-Hunter asked.

'No, they're not in it,' Mr Daunders was sure. 'They're just a couple of sycophants. Anyway, Somerled was paying them. He wouldn't be paying them if they were in the gang. They would have their share of whatever money's going. Whatever it comes from.'

'Gambling?' suggested Mr Baillie-Hunter.

'I hardly think so. What kind of odds with the money a schoolboy has would let Savage win four pounds?'

Mr Baillie-Hunter finished his mid-morning coffee with his headmaster and returned to his class for a poetry lesson. He was reading to them *Lord Ullin's Daughter* and acting it well, changing his voice to be the chief of Ulva's isle, the boatman and Lord Ullin, and even the raging storm itself. He ended solemnly in a good rolling Scotch voice.

> '*'Twas vain! The loud waves lashed the shore,*
> *Return or aid preventing.*
> *The waters wild went o'er his child,*
> *And he was left lamenting.*'

He indicated the rise and fall of the waves by an undulation of his right hand, and in the sorrowful hush that followed his dramatic reading he looked round the class with gratification. He knew he had a good delivery, and he found a certain pleasure in giving such a touching rendering of corny ballads that children were thrilled to unshed tears. He expected to see here and there a hand furtively brushing a wet eye. Then he exploded at the dry-eyed inattention of a boy in the back row.

A minute later he barged into Mr Daunder's room and slapped down a dozen or so bits of paper on the headmaster's desk.

'I just found Wedderburn playing with – with these,' he gulped, agonized.

'What are they?' said Mr Daunders, putting the stock book aside. He had an annual return to make to the office, and he was puzzled to see the stock book showing him as having a piano more on hand than he thought he had. For any other item he would have balanced the discrepancy in the usual way by putting '1' under the 'Consumed' column, but he wasn't sure he could properly claim to have consumed a piano.

'They're bits of a five-pound note,' Mr Baillie-Hunter moaned. 'All the bits! Wedderburn was playing with them.'

'Oh, Jesus Christ!' Mr Daunders breathed devoutly, a pious ejaculation for divine assistance, his elbow on his desk, his brow on his hand, the stock book and the mysterious extra piano forgotten.

'He was doing it as a jig-saw puzzle,' Mr Baillie-Hunter complained miserably. 'You see, it's all there! Somebody has cut it in little pieces. You see how clever it is.'

He fitted two or three of the geometric fragments together. 'It was just a jig-saw to Wedderburn, it wasn't money, it was a puzzle. He says he found it inside his poetry book. You see, I don't let them keep their poetry books. I give them out when I take poetry. So anybody could have left them there if he's telling the truth. And he knows we can't prove he isn't.'

'We'll have to get to the bottom of this,' Mr Daunders muttered, and rubbed his palm wearily across his aching eyes. 'This can't go on. Ten-shilling notes, pound notes, a five-pound note. Where is it going to end?'

He brooded.

'Yes, as I told you, I've got a very strong feeling there's too much money floating around this school. Do you know, I've had about a dozen parents up lately. Complaining. Their children can't sleep at night, or when they do they have nightmares. And they're off their food. They seem to think Jasper's frightening the weans. Then they say, "Oh it must be all these sweeties they're eating between meals". But they can't tell me where the money's coming from to buy sweets to that extent. They talk as if it was my job to stop them eating sweets!'

He brooded again.

'Garson!' he cried, slapping his desk so hard that the phone tinkled for a moment or two. 'I've got it. Garson knows the answer.'

'Garson wouldn't be mixed up in anything dishonest,' Mr Baillie-Hunter objected indignantly. 'Garson's a good boy. He grasped decimals right away.'

'Maybe so,' said Mr Daunders. 'But he's in on this money epidemic I'm sure. That's why Savage gave him a beating. Garson knows where all this money's coming from, and he was going to talk. I'll make him talk all right! You get him in here now.'

But Garson wouldn't talk. He still believed that what Percy was doing was wrong, he was still afraid a day of reckoning must come, and he still wanted no part of it. But he was quite clear in his own mind that the discovery of the hoard would never come through him. He had his own code. He was loyal. Loyalty was all that was left to him, even though it was loyalty to a gang that had never completely accepted him. He was worried about Percy most of all. He believed Percy should have taken his side against Savage and not been so neutral, but he still loved him. Percy was the leader and the organizer. He was the eldest. Whoever had to pay one day, Percy would have to pay most. And he wasn't going to have Percy's punishment on his conscience. Since it had to come sooner or later let it come later, through the inevitable gathering of circumstance, not because of any words he ever spoke. He had been long prepared to cope with an interrogator who knew much more than Mr Daunders.

'Now you didn't just fight about nothing,' Mr Daunders kept at him, stubbornly drilling through his stony silence. 'Something must have started it. Tell me what it was.'

Garson recognized it was time to answer. His fingertips went to the bruised and swollen bone under his eye.

'It was a private matter,' he said.

'How private?' Mr Daunders asked. 'You can surely tell me. I'm trying to help you.'

'My family,' said Garson, warmed to a confidence by the old man's kind wheedling voice.

'What do you mean, your family?' Mr Daunders pushed at him.

'He-he-he insulted my mother,' Garson answered, his rosy cheeks rosier, his engaging stammer appearing for a moment. 'So I hit him and he hit me back, and we-we-we started to fight. It was a fair fight.'

'I see,' Mr Daunders murmured, as embarrassed as the boy. He felt he had blundered. He should have known better than to go on once Garson mentioned his family. You never knew what scandals you were going to stumble on if you asked too many questions about a boy's family in this school. He remembered the muddle he had failed to sort out when he tried to discover why a boy was called Addison, his mother was called Mrs Mappin, and the man she was living with, whose name was on the doorplate, was called Tanner. Mr Tanner called one morning after it was proposed to send Addison to a special school, a school for the mentally handicapped, and Mr Daunders tactfully queried his relationship to the boy.

'Oh, I'm one of his parents,' Mr Tanner answered lightly. 'In a sort of way, you see.'

'I see,' said Mr Daunders, wondering who Mr Mappin

was if there ever was one, and what had happened to Mr Addison.

The trivial incident had been a lesson to him, but he still felt he should probe Garson. He still felt there was more to the fight with Garson than a schoolboy's routine insult to a classmate's parent. He remained convinced Savage was afraid of what Garson knew and had given him a beating to keep him quiet. He believed if he kept on asking questions he would come to the real sore, distinct from the wound about an insulted mother though perhaps connected with it.

'And what did he say about your mother that annoyed you so much?' he tried.

Garson looked at him and trembled with a strange pity. The man seemed to want to be shocked. He surrendered. He would repeat just what he had suffered and let this grown-up suffer too. Why should he bear the cruelty of the world alone? But he couldn't use Savage's words. He answered in the book-English a bright Scots schoolboy uses when he talks respectfully to his teachers.

'He accused my mother of eloping with a Negro,' he said.

'Oh dear,' said Mr Daunders sadly. He knew a dead-end when he came to it. But he couldn't stop worrying away like a dog at a bone. He turned the topic over and attacked it another way.

'You're sure it wasn't because you knew something about Savage that he doesn't want anyone else to know?'

For all its directness the question missed the target. Garson certainly felt guilty about the money, but the money meant Percy and the whole Brotherhood, not specifically Savage. He answered with a candour that was totally convincing because it was genuine.

'I don't know anything about Savage.'

'He's not afraid of anything you know?'

That came a little nearer. Garson was uneasy for a moment. He wondered if Old Daundy could possibly have got on to the money in the cellar. He put the idea away. If he knew about the money in the cellar he wouldn't be wasting time asking a lot of silly questions. As for the question just put to him, he couldn't see why Savage should be afraid of him when the rest of the Brotherhood knew all he knew. Surely Savage knew he would keep the oath as faithfully as the rest of them.

'There's nothing I know that other folk don't know,' he answered carefully. 'Savage has no reason to be afraid of me.'

Mr Daunders let him go, but unwillingly. He felt he had neared the brink of the abyss where the mystery was buried.

It was a day of interrogation for Garson. His father started too after their silent evening meal together. From the casual way he spoke the boy guessed he had been thinking about it all day.

'You never told me what you were fighting about anyway. What started it?'

What made grown-ups ask questions they wouldn't like to hear answered, the boy wondered. He had had enough. If he could tell Mr Daunders he could tell his father. It was only right people should get what they asked for.

'Savage said my mother ran away with a darkie,' he said sullenly, and waited for it, ready to cower. And indeed his father's hand went up before the words were fully spoken. The boy moved round the kitchen table to safety. His father put his hand back in his pocket and let him be.

'That's not true,' he said walking from the kitchen sink to the kitchen door and back again, rubbing his nose, rubbing his lips.

The boy watched him alertly and waited.

'It's not true,' his father repeated. 'That's gossip. I know what they say. But it's not true. Your mother didn't run away with anybody.'

'What did she do?' the boy demanded, his battered face twisted to choke the tears that the memory of Savage's taunt brought back to his eyes. 'Why is she not here?'

'Aye, as far as you're concerned she just disappeared,' his

father muttered, still walking up and down, still rubbing his face and thrusting his fingers through his hair in a private misery. 'That's all I know myself.'

'Why?' said the boy, determined to keep at it. He was going to find out something he wanted to know, he was sure of it. People had asked him too many questions. It was his turn.

'Because she – because she wouldn't do what I told her,' said his father. He was started, his tongue was loosened after years of silence. He had to tell himself now, not just his son. 'She took a job on the buses. She was a conductress. I didn't want her to. But I let her do it because she said she needed the money for new this and new that. I don't know what the hell she didn't want. She wanted new curtains, that was all to begin with. Just work for a wee while, she said. Then she wanted a washing-machine, then she wanted a television, then she wanted a fridge. It was going to go on for ever. I told her to stop. Her place was in the house. But oh no, her place was wherever she liked. She liked being out working. The house was just dull, she was nobody's skivvy. She was going to go on working just as long as it pleased her. I ordered her. A man's the head of his own family. But she wouldn't obey me.'

'You sent her away!' the boy saw the truth of it, and he was gripped by a hatred of his father's masculine authority.

'I told her to come back into the house or leave the house,' his father admitted.

'And where does the darkie come in?' the boy asked, feeling a black cloud between himself and his father.

'There's no darkie,' said his father wearily, resting from his walking up and down and standing with his hands wide apart on the kitchen table as he looked across at his bitter son with unhappy eyes. 'Your mother's driver was a West Indian, that was all. She was always on the same shift with him. They got on but that was all. He's been in this house since your mother went away. He tried to help. He's got his own wife and family. She never ran away with him. That's nonsense. People said that because they were pals but it's not true. Any conductress on the buses is pally with her driver.'

'But you must know where she is,' the boy complained. Now the darkie was explained he didn't matter. What mattered was that his mother had been allowed to stay away. 'You could find out easily enough. You could find her depot and get her address.'

'She changed her depot.'

'You could find out.'

'I'm not going to run after anybody,' his father shouted. 'She made her choice. She wants to work, well, she can work. If she wouldn't agree her place is here, then this is no place for her.'

He stared down at the table, his eyes on a dirty plate of ham and eggs.

'I'm sorry,' he conceded to his son. 'Maybe she's sorry. I don't know. But there's some things can never be put right. But that's a lot of nonsense about a darkie. There was nothing between them. Just because she left me when she was working with a coloured driver some people liked to make up a story and they ended up believing it themselves. But it's only a story. That wasn't the trouble. Your mother never had that fault. It was just she said she could help the house by working and I told her she could help it better by being the housewife. I told her if I couldn't keep a wife I didn't deserve a wife. My mother never had to go out to work. And she had a hard time of it. My father never had the job I have. That's what it was about.'

'I want my mother back,' the boy cried, but only to himself. He couldn't say it aloud.

The father waved a hand over the dejected tea-table.

'Come on! You get this table redd and get these dishes washed and stop greeting.'

'You did what was wrong,' the boy muttered, moving to his chore with the speed of a snail. 'I'm not greeting.'

'Maybe I did,' his father answered. 'Well, you're damn near greeting. You'll have to learn not to. It doesn't get ye anywhere. Maybe I did, but sometimes you've got to do what's wrong to be right.'

The boy stopped listening. He was thinking. What kind of a house was this, where he had to do the washing and cleaning and shopping and make up the laundry and do the cooking? If his mother had stayed at home he could have lived like other boys instead of having to live like a girl. A rebellion was gathering in him. The road to open insurrection appeared before him as he lay snivelling in bed that night, and when he was doing his paper-rake the next evening he loitered on the stairhead and looked at the advertising pages of the *Evening Citizen*. If his mother had gone away because she wanted to get more money then a promise of plenty would surely bring her back. Money seemed to be the eternal question and the universal answer.

He was the only member of the Brotherhood still working after school hours. Everybody else had given up delivering papers, milk, and rolls, and going round with the fruit-lorry or the man with the float of coal-briquettes. Why should they break the law forbidding schoolboys to work, just to earn a few bob, when they had pounds for the lifting? They despised the tips they had once gloated over, but Frank Garson still depended on them. His father gave him little, and what he gave him he gave irregularly. The boy had no grudge. He handed over his wages every week with pride. He couldn't help being faithful. It was the way God had made him. But he kept all his tips. They were his own the way he saw it.

And now he pouted thoughtfully, childish brows furrowed, as he read the small ad rates. His father never bought an evening paper, so he felt he could proceed in safety. The prices interested him. It was like sending a telegram. Intimations (Births, Marriages, Deaths) two and six a line; Property, three shillings. Holiday Guide, three shillings, Situations Vacant, three shillings, Personal (Private), four shillings, and Personal (Trade), four and six a line. He wrote his appeal four times on a sheet of jotter-paper before he got it right, and asked Percy to let him use the portable typewriter to type it out fair. He knew Percy was too much of a gentleman to ask what he was typing. He did it in the cellar, alone in a corner, before the start of a mid-week service. GARSON, he jabbed with one finger, and went slowly on, searching the keyboard grimly for the necessary letters. HELEN, he assembled. *Come home. Admit was wrong. Money no bother. Frank has loads. Bob.*

He knew his father's Christian name was Robert and he supposed his mother must have called him Bob, but he couldn't hear her in his mind. She seemed to belong to that other world he had lived in when he was young. Now he was old, living in a real world, a hard, solid world where things were enemies. He felt he was trying to call up a ghost. But for all his doubts he went to the *Citizen* office alone, wandered round fearlessly till he found the right counter, and tholed the squint glance of the clerk who counted the words. It cost him sixteen shillings. He paid it with a pound note Percy had thrust on him to make up for not giving him better support against Savage. He took it as a gift from Percy. It came privately from Percy's pocket, not from the chest in front of the Brotherhood, so he claimed before his conscience that he still hadn't taken any share of the hoard. It would be time enough to demand his rights in it when his mother came home.

CHAPTER TEN

Helen Garson was working the Yoker–Auchenshuggle route with a new driver two nights later. Her husband was right when he had told their son the West Indian had nothing to do with her leaving home, but she still kept up with her old driver. She had to have some friends, and she visited the West Indian and his wife about once a month and had the distraction of sitting for an evening with a happy family where she felt welcome. Apart from that, she was a lonely woman, determined to like living alone. She bashed on, doing her best not to grieve for her man and her boy and her old home in Bethel Street, and she was doing as well as could be expected until two things upset her.

The first thing was Percy got on her bus about ten o'clock at the Hielenman's Umbrella, and the sight of him reminded her of Bethel Street and that reminded her of all she was stubbornly forgetting. He wasn't alone. He was escorting a girl, a long-legged, wide-skirted, pony-tailed, large-breasted, gum-chewing, big-eyed teenager. She knew him at once but he didn't know her. He was only a boy at school the last time she saw him and now he was like a young man, so stylishly dressed that he looked slightly odd. He sat in the back seat upstairs, holding his girl's hand and their brows touched as they mooned together the whole journey. She grued a little at the sight of them, for she was an anti-romantic, and the girl seemed to her anyway a stupid-faced doll who would be none the worse for a scrubbing and a haircut. Percy wore the gawky look he had always worn, but he was wearing it with a difference now. Instead of the gawkiness of a backward schoolboy he was showing the gawkiness of the male animal reaching towards the female for the first time and not quite sure how to set about it. She was glad to see them get off at Partick Cross. They linked arms when they stepped on the pavement and she sent a sniff of contempt after them.

'He never was very bright,' she thought as she rattled upstairs and down, breezily collecting her fares and tyrannizing the passengers as only a Glasgow bus-conductress can. 'He was aye kind of glaikit and he doesn't seem to have improved any. Seeing a girl home at his age! And where did he get the money to dress like that? I bet he hasn't got two pennies to rub together. I don't know how they do it nowadays, courting before they're right out of school. And he's left himself with some journey back home too, the silly fool! It's no' a girlfriend he's got, it's a pen-pal, staying that distance from him. The things they'll do when they think they're in love! Ah well, they'll get a rude awakening one day and hell mend them. All they think of is sex, they're sex-mad, these kids nowadays. The way she sat pushing her breasts up to him, must have been pads she was wearing, the little bitch. Ach, they'll learn one day, when they've rent to pay and light to pay and coal to get and weans to feed and clothe.'

She was so annoyed with Percy for coming on her bus and raising ghosts that she made up for it by tearing him and his girl to pieces all the way along Dumbarton road to the end of the line.

Then at the lying-in time there the second thing happened to upset her. It was worse than the first, much worse. She saw her son's small ad in the paper. It was just a piece of bad luck, for she never bought an evening paper. She happened to see this one because on the last lap of the journey she left her bus for a moment and bought two pokes of chips, one for her driver and one for herself. It was a bad shift they were on, and they had got the habit of buying chips to give them a filling bite between the end of one run and the start of another. The Italian who owned the fish-and-chip shop always served her at once, no matter who else was waiting, and she was back on her bus before the passengers knew she had left it. She handed the chips in to the driver. They would keep warmer in his cabin than on her platform.

When the empty bus lay at the terminus she sat downstairs facing her driver, and since he was the strong silent type she occupied herself reading one of the sheets of newspaper Enrico had wrapped round the two pokes.

'That's last night's paper you're reading,' her driver remarked detachedly, recognizing a headline.

'You don't expect him to wrap the chips in tonight's paper, do you?' she answered crossly, and turned the page.

She gazed amongst the births, marriages and deaths, delving into the chips with coin-grimed fingers while her driver ate his way steadily through the other poke.

'Harry didn't put much salt on them the night,' he commented.

'You're hell of a talkative all of a sudden,' she retorted. 'Just you go get them tomorrow night then and you tell him that!'

'I don't like a lot of salt,' he said, after brooding over her answer.

'I see there's an awful lot of shorthand-typists wanted,' she muttered.

'Ach, they're no' well paid they girls,' he said. 'You're getting more than them, even without your overtime.'

She turned from the situations vacant to the ads for second-hand furniture, vacuum cleaners, fur coats and tape-recorders.

'What do people buy all these things for if they're that damned hard-up they've got to sell them?' she asked peevishly. 'They buy them the one day and want to sell them the next. Aye, they're all as good as new according to the advert. Aye, I don't think!'

She was just going to crumple the paper and dump it in the litter-bin at the bus stop when she saw her married name in small capitals at the foot of a column.

The whole thing was a sheer fluke, a pure accident, a fortuitous concatenation of circumstances. That Enrico had happened to use that page to put round the chips and that she happened to see the ad at all, was the kind of coincidence that happens every day in the real world that God created but is condemned as far-fetched in the work of a novelist, as if God wasn't the greatest novelist of all.

She frowned. She scowled. She stared. She read it three times and squinted over at her driver. He was lighting the remainder of the cigarette he had started at the other end of the route. He didn't seem to be watching her and she didn't tell him what she had seen. She wasn't a woman given to confidences. She tore out the ad roughly and stuffed it quickly in her pocket.

'Are you going after another job?' her driver asked casually.

'You don't miss much, do you?' she answered, crumpling the paper viciously.

In a little while she was busy collecting fares again as her bus weaved east, and when the top deck was full and she had five standing downstairs she stopped anybody else from boarding, barring them with the lucid command always given by Glasgow bus-conductresses in such circumstances, 'Come on, get off!'

She was too harassed to think any more of Percy, who had anyway been displaced by the advertisement she had seen, and she didn't know that when she passed Partick Cross he was standing with his girl in the back-close of a grey tenement north of her route. The back-close is that part of the close that lies beyond the stairway to the flats and leads to the back-court. Since it usually turns at an angle from the front-close and can't be seen from the street it is the site of countless Glasgow courtships and seductions. Some write of beds and sofas, some sing of the green corn-fields and acres of rye, some tumble panting in the hay, but Glasgow's sons and lovers have the back-close.

For all he had a pride in possessing the refinement of a true poet Percy was insensible to the drabness of the setting. He was in a state. It didn't matter that the midden was only fifteen paces away across the back-court nor that the brown paint of the close was chipped, peeled, and scarred with obscure incisions by the pocket-knives of schoolboys. He was exalted. He had been aching for a girl and now he had one. He had one all to himself, all alone, against the wall though not against her will. He was trembling on the brink. His curiosity was as wide and burning as his ignorance, but it was the way girls dressed disturbed him more than the girls themselves. Indeed the girls he saw every day left him inwardly as cold as a Scots summer. It was advertisements for nylons, brassieres and girdles made his heart quicken, toilet soaps and deodorants told him of breasts and armpits, and foam petticoats under wide skirts whispered to him a warming suggestion of the unseen thighs above the calves and the instep arched by high heels. They all created a mysterious world of elegance, freshness, cleanliness and softness that he longed to enter and embrace, a world not inhabited by the girls he saw every day. But Sophy had long legs and a wide skirt, she had a bust like a girl in a television advert, her hair was glossy, she smelt of soap and something else, so it was Sophy he wanted.

Of course, his curiosity concerned anatomy as well as underwear. Faces never moved him, for the face was always visible. But he would saunter slowly past the window of a ladies' gown shop in Sauchiehall street, squinting in a fluster at the naked wax models of women, and pretend he wasn't looking at the breasts, belly and thighs at all, his big feet pointing north and south as he ambled west. Not sure of what he had seen he would turn back at a decent distance and stroll past the window again, his head hot with guilt, but he never dared stop and stare and get it right once and for all.

And now at last he had a girl of his own. Now at last he could come to grips with the problem and be satisfied with the answer. He had survived the first stage of saying goodnight at the bus-stop. He had been given a pass-mark and allowed to enter the second degree of saying goodnight at the close-mouth. Tonight Sophy seemed ready to let him graduate. She let him edge her into the back-close and when they were there she put her handbag on the ground to leave her hands free if he tried to make love to her.

She was a very junior waitress in a cheap restaurant, a rough eating-house where he went for a midday meal when he first gave up his job. Then he began going there for morning coffee because it wasn't so busy before lunch, then for afternoon tea too when it was quiet again, and he could sit and look at her in peace. She couldn't help getting to know him by sight, and when she moved around and Percy sat admiring her bright legs and her hips under her black dress she answered him with a little smirk of a smile over her shoulder. He spoke to her at last with all the confidence in the world, depending on the money in the cellar to see him through all difficulties. Without telling her a direct lie he let her think he was a student. He thought that would explain why he could spend so much time just sitting around. He let her see he had money by tipping her absurdly every day and making a show of opening his wallet to pay his bill so that she could see the wad of notes inside.

Naturally she agreed at once to go out with him, but for all his money he never took her anywhere special. He had the money all right, but not the knowledge gained only from experience how to spend it. He was intimidated by the uppish look of expensive places, with a commissionaire at the door, and he never dared cross the threshold. A frugal eater and a non-drinker, he could move only within a narrow circle of cafes and cinemas. It didn't bother Sophy. A cinema in town and a box of chocolates were luxury enough to her. She wouldn't have been comfortable drinking cocktails in a hotel lounge. Percy suited her, except when he told her he was a poet. Still, she got over it quickly. She supposed a boy had a right to at least one oddity and she believed poets were great lovers. She waited for the great lover when they were embraced in the back-close.

As for Percy, he had dreamed of this hour and this solitude so long and so often that the reality of it was but a dim substitute for the ideal. Yet because it was the nearest he had come to his desire he felt himself on the verge of great deeds and great discoveries. He believed he was thrilled, and he was. He was wandering in the pathways of the moon, guided by a celestial light that illumed her remote beauty while he drowned in the deep mournfulness of a love not yet made known and satisfied. He gazed at Sophy's brow and cheeks and the curve of her throat and his worship grew and grew. He was in bliss. The light of consciousness went out and his heart vibrated in a fecund darkness that promised the unutterable satisfaction he deserved.

With an inscrutable smile Sophy spoke.

'Did you ever think of writing a pome about me?' she

asked in a voice as if some tender soul imprisoned within her was asking the question. After all, she was only seventeen, though she had been kissed often enough. 'I mean, when you're writing your pomes do you ever do one to me? Just how you see me, I mean, when you sit watching me serve the tables and saying what you think about me?'

'Well, I did start something,' he admitted, red-faced but encouraged by her interest in his work. 'It's a sort of song. You know, what Rabbie Burns used to write, that kinda thing.'

He chanted huskily.

'Doh, soh, me, re-doh.'

After a nervous swallow he went on, incanting his composition to her in the development of a simple melody.

> 'Darling, you must know
> How I dream of you
> Morning, noon and night,
> You make the world seem bright,
> Fill me with delight.
> Sweetheart, kiss me gaily
> As I play my ukelele,
> Then just hold me tight,
> Hold me tight and love me right,
> And be mine tonight.'

'That's lovely,' she beamed the brightness of her smile in the dim corner while his hands fidgeted up and down her flanks. 'I like the way it rhymes. You could sell that.'

'Oh, I don't write for money,' he said proudly.

'But it doesn't say much about me. I mean, it doesn't describe me. I'm just not there, am I?'

'Well, that's not the point,' he defended his lyric. 'You see, a poet writes about his emotions, not so much what he sees like, it's what he feels. That's what matters to him, what he feels.'

He felt her hips and back with wandering hands and she squirmed in a movement ambiguously encouraging and disapproving.

'Yes, but there's not many girls with hair like me, or my complexion,' she suggested. 'Then there's my eyes. Did you never think of writing about my eyes, for instance?'

'No, it wasn't so much your eyes,' he answered, a crease in his brow as if he were thinking.

'Well, what was it then?' she persisted. 'What was it first attracted you to me?'

'It was the way you walked, you know, the way you go round the tables,' he said. He didn't want to say it was her legs. He talked around it.

She made a low humming sound of acknowledgement, staring over his shoulder at the scribbling on the opposite wall as if she was trying to read what was there.

'Did you ever hear of Shelley?' he asked. He felt he had a duty to educate her. 'He was a great poet if you like, a rebel. That's what I am. I don't agree with the world as it is today. I mean to say. I've read all his works. Do you know him?'

'No, I can't say I do,' she conceded. His hands were at rest now he was going to teach her all about Shelley, and she wasn't sure if she would have preferred his tongue to be at rest instead.

'There's a smashing wee pome of his I learned off by heart,' he said relentlessly. 'Would you like to hear it?'

'I don't mind I'm sure,' she said patiently. She had been out with all kinds of boys in her short sweet life. She had learnt to be accommodating.

'See!' he declared abruptly, and she was reminded of a Scots comic she had once heard say, 'See? See me! I don't like fish!'

He gulped and went on in a canting voice.

> *'The mountains kiss the heavens*
> *And the waves clasp one another.*
> *And the moonbeams kiss the sea.*
> *What is all this kissing worth*
> *If you don't kiss me?'*

'That's nice, I like that,' she breathed, and they kissed. He wasn't very good at it and she felt he needed practice.

'That's Shelley, that is,' he broke off. He couldn't kiss and talk and he had to talk. He was getting scared at his own state. He was there on the brink, afraid the dip would be too cold. Talking would put off the embarrassing need for action. 'It's called love's philosophy.'

'Oh, yes, of course,' she answered intelligently.

'It goes on,' he said.

And he went on, his hands on her hips inside her open coat while hers dangled daintily over his narrow shoulders.

> *'The fountains mingle with the river*
> *And the river with the ocean,*
> *The winds of heaven mix for ever*
> *With a rare emotion.*
> *Nothing in the world is single,*
> *All things by a law divine*
> *In one another's being mingle,*
> *So why not you with mine?'*

He ended throatily, appealingly.

'I don't like that,' she said severely, staring beyond him again. 'I don't think it's very nice.'

She wriggled. He was pressing too hard against her. She squirmed loose and stepped past him, right shoulder forward her body very straight and her head up as if she was doing the side-stepping movement in a reel.

He managed to grab the tail of her coat just as she reached the bend in the close under the gaslight. She was halted. Percy tugged and she pulled and they wrestled. They finished up panting in the back-close again, only this time they were against the opposite wall. So Percy won. Or Sophy let him win, for who would dare argue that the parallelogram of forces represents the resultant of a lovers' scuffle?

'Don't be daft,' he complained, standing over her with his long arms on either side of her drooping shoulders so that she was barred from escape. 'What did you want to run away like that for?'

'Cause I didn't like what you were insinuating,' she said firmly.

'I wasn't insinuating nothing,' he answered, all hurt. 'It was Shelley I was saying.'

'I still don't like it,' she tossed her head.

'But there's nothing wrong in it,' he argued. 'It's perfectly natural. That's what Shelley was saying. If two people love each other like you and me—'

His arms came closer in his eagerness to confine her.

'I wish you'd lay off the subject,' she muttered, scowling darkly in the dimness.

'Why?' he demanded, and his arms went round her like the coils of a boa-constrictor. Inspired by a confused recollection of a novel by Lawrence he had tried to read he was proud of his wholesome maturity and maleness and he longed to reach the dark roots of her being and quicken her. 'We should act according to our impulses, it's the only natural thing to do, if a man's to be a man.'

'I thought you was a nice boy,' she complained, struggling again.

He was worse than he had been. The wrestling-match at the bend of the close had raised his temperature to boiling point and he was in a state again.

'Oh, Sophy, please,' he groaned, an asthmatic bull in a grassless meadow. 'I think you're wonderful. I love you. I want you.'

She didn't even pretend to be impressed. She sent a little signal of scepticism through her nose, a maidenly snort of disbelief, but he blundered on. He felt he was face to face with death, the death of his hopes for an initiation with Sophy. He didn't want to die, ever, and he was panic-stricken in case he died wondering.

'Come on, be a sport, let me!' he pleaded, as hoarse as an NCO after his first day taking a squad in the square.

He wound round her to crush her squirming body in a heroic hug, but she ducked, side-stepped, and stood free of him. He was bang up against the scarred brown paintwork on the wall while Sophy stood at his side with one hand on her hip and the other caressing her pony-tail. But he still wasn't beaten. He was only provoked. He went on blundering.

'I can make it worth your while,' he declared, staggering from the unwelcoming wall. He delved into the pocket inside his new sports jacket (best Harris tweed, heather mixture pattern, fourteen guineas in Carswell's), fumbled with his pocket book, opened it trembling, and brought out a five-pound note, another five-pound note, waved them before her astounded young eyes.

'You can have them! You can have them both! I don't care, there's plenty more where they came from!'

He was teetering there, certain he was going to gain her, and then her little hand darted. First in a vertical flash it scattered his precious wallet and then it came back on the horizontal plane and slapped him hard across the face. (Mrs Maguire on the ground floor stood with the teapot over her cup and breathed nervously, 'What was that?')

Percy put his hand to his cheek as if to make sure it was really his face she had smacked.

'Well, I like that!' Sophy flared. 'So that's the kind of girl you think I am! Just right here and now, eh? Just like that? Do you think I'm mad? And if you've got that kind of money to throw away what the hell are you bothering about me at all for, tell me that! You don't need to come slobbering round me if you want to buy it. You know where to go or it's high bloody time you did. Well, I like that! You and your po'try. And I don't know what you're doing with all that money anyway, a fella that's no' working. I've a good mind to tell my brother about you.'

Her inflated little bosom heaved, she flared and sputtered at him. Then she picked up her handbag and marched off. No side-slip this time, but a military quickstep, and Percy was left alone with his smarting face. He stood bleak and frozen in the twilight of the back-close, heard Sophy's high heels tattoo upstairs, heard her knock at her door on the second storey of the three, heard the door open and the door bang. She was gone, gone for ever. He nearly wept.

But perhaps her brother was in. There was no time to waste in tears. He picked up his wallet in a flurry, put the fivers back inside as he hurried through the front-close and ran to the nearest bus-stop.

It was all very well for Shelley. He could say it and get it printed in his immortal works and even in the *Golden Treasury*. But Shelley didn't have to deal with these narrow-minded waitresses who had no appreciation of love's philosophy. He worked hard on a grudge against Sophy as he waited splay-footed and nervous for a bus to come, one hand inside his jacket fondling his wallet as a talisman. He didn't care which bus he got so long as it took him away from the scene of his Waterloo. He suddenly felt hungry, and a shattering thought lashed his already turbulent mind.

'I'll have to find somewhere else to eat now!' he lamented to the bus-stop standard, and tutted to the night air at the nuisance of it. He felt himself wronged and humiliated. After the way she had mentioned her brother he would have to disappear for good so far as Sophy was concerned. He had made a mistake.

'Ach, maybe she was right,' he thought generously arguing against his fabricated grudge, for he took a pride in always seeing at least two sides to any question. 'Maybe it was a mistake to offer her money. But I was desperate. I should have kept it till after.'

By the time he was speeding home on the bus his brain was empty. It was tired of fretting about Sophy and the absurd failure to seduce her. The stranger drifted in to fill the vacuum.

'Oh, dear! There's him to worry about!' he remembered in misery. 'He's a menace, he is! I wonder where he's got to.'

Stumbling on a rhyme he brooded about a poem in which a stranger was a danger. He thought out the first two lines.

'Within life's vale of tears I face one danger
That makes my blood run cold, a questioning stranger—'

But he couldn't go on. His headache began to bother him again, his stomach quivered, turned, tied itself in painful knots. He was frightened again. Sophy's brother and the stranger merged into one cloud darkening his future, disturbing his peace of mind.

CHAPTER ELEVEN

Mrs Phinn's daily duties as a school-cleaner were in two spells. She went in at six in the morning before the school opened and worked till a quarter to nine, and she went back at four o'clock in the afternoon when the school was dismissed and worked till six in the evening. She did it with a grudge. She hated being a poor widow who had to do a menial job for a few shillings to pay her way, and a hardup way it was. She resented being under the eye of the janitor for clocking in in the morning and clocking out at tea-time, because she despised him as an interloper. He would never have got the job if her husband hadn't been found dead in the cellar the day after his brother was killed in a car-crash on the Glasgow–Edinburgh road, the notorious A8. And he didn't strike her as being a janitor in the true tradition. He wasn't like her husband, serious, clever and experienced. He was a flippant, scruffy, inexpert little man, always calling in a plumber or a joiner for jobs her man would have done himself as a matter of course. And he knew next to nothing about janitor's stock or janitor's requisitions. He could never say, as her husband had said in all truth, that although he was only the janitor he was just as important to the school as any headmaster. Her husband knew his job. This fellow didn't. He didn't even know his place. He was chatty with the headmaster and familiar with the cleaners.

'Well, with some of them,' she complained to Percy, not that he was listening. 'That Mrs Winters in particular is never out of his room. I don't see how she can be doing her job right, the time she spends sitting in there drinking tea. They think I don't know. She's some widow, that one. Made up to kill. Out at six in the morning with her powder on thick and her lipstick on like a chorus girl. I don't know what he thinks he's up to. She's no' as young as she makes out to be. Her hair's dyed for one thing. And he's got a wife of his own anyway. She calls him by his first name. Imagine that! None of the cleaners ever dared call your father by his first name when he was on duty. But this little upstart never wears a hat. Your father used to polish the badge in his hat every night. He looked the part. He knew how to hold himself. He knew how to speak to cleaners. But all these things is dying out now. Everybody's equal. It's all wrong.'

She crossed to the main gate at six o'clock the morning after her son had kept his chastity and her body trembled with longing for the sleep the alarm had broken. Yet it was a fine summer morning, the sky above the tall tenements was blue and unclouded, and the pigeons were already talking to each other in the high roof of the sandstone school. She grudged feeling it was good to be alive after all, but she felt it, and her awakening senses granted to her weary body that it was better to be up and doing on such a lovely morning than lying in a lazy bed. She was just coming really awake, approaching the gate, when a man at the corner of Bethel Street and Tulip Place whistled to her. She was affronted. She was wearing old stockings, her bare head showed her greying hair, and anyway six o'clock in the morning, even if it was a lovely morning, was no time for a man to be accosting a woman. Her head reared and her small thin body stiffened, dignity and alarm fighting for control of her. She glanced obliquely at the whistler, just to see what kind of man he was. He came quickly towards her, beckoning her over anxiously. She stood still and waited. She wasn't going to walk to any man. Let him come to her. The janitor would hear her if she screamed.

'Mrs Phinn?' he asked civilly.

118

She didn't deny it.

'I'm the man that drove the car,' he said. 'You know, Sammy's car.'

She looked at him hard. She didn't believe in ghosts at any time, certainly not at six o'clock on a summer morning.

'He was killed,' she said. 'They both were killed, Sammy and the man that was driving him.'

'Aye, on the Friday, but I mean on the Thursday. It was me that drove the car on the Thursday, that's what I mean, on the Thursday night.'

He smiled wisely to her, showing two yellow fangs, but she was more taken by a pink line from his nose to his jawbone, the scar of a razor-slash.

'I don't know what you're talking about, I'm sorry,' she answered, her head up and back from him as if he was a bad egg she had just cracked.

'Who are ye kidding, missis?' he complained, not so civil now. 'You know damn fine what Sammy was up to the Thursday night afore he was killed.'

'He was up to no good if I know him,' she snapped. 'He always was up to no good.'

'He was up to a lot of good that night,' the stranger smiled again. 'And he saw your man on the Friday morning afore he went to Edinburgh. You know that, don't you?'

'I'm afraid I don't,' she snubbed him. 'I can assure you my man wanted as little to do as possible with his brother even if they was twins.'

'Did Hamish no' tell you what he did with it all?' he kept at her.

'All what?' she asked impatiently. 'I've got my work to go to, I can't stand here wasting time talking to you, when I don't even know who you are anyway.'

'I've told you who I am,' he said, his hands out with the palms up. 'I'm one of Sammy's crowd. It was me drove the car, and I got nothing for it. No, he tells me to wait, just wait. It'll be all right in a month or two. Then he goes and gets killed and here's me still waiting. Somebody must know. You must know. Because Sammy saw your man right after it.'

'I assure you I don't know,' she insisted, very dignified with him, talking with a bogus accent to let him know she was a respectable woman who knew nothing of her criminal brother-in-law. 'I can assure you I've no idea what you're talking about.'

She looked towards the gate and wondered if she could run that far and get into the school before this strange man assaulted her.

'Don't give us that,' he said roughly, his palm lightly under her elbow, ready to clutch her if she moved. 'You must know. Look, Sammy was coming back from Edinburgh when he had that smash, wasn't he? And he'd been to see the jelly-man, hadn't he? Don't argue. I know. And he gave him fifty quid on account, but that was in fivers from another bank. So he's still waiting too. The bloke with him that was killed, he went inside with Sammy, but he had nothing on him when he was killed. There's nobody had nothing. So where is it? It's a hell of a lot of money to be lying about.'

'If you're trying to insinuate that my brother-in-law stole some money and gave it to my husband to keep for him, you're mistaken,' Mrs Phinn locuted at him. 'And I can assure you I know nothing about any money. Do I look as if I had anything to do with money? Do you think I'd be out here at this time in the morning going to sweep floors if I had any money?'

'That's no' the point,' he countered. 'You couldny use the kind of money I'm talking about. It would only scare folk like you. You wouldny know whit to do wi' it. All you've got to do is tell me what Sammy fixed up wi' Hamish and I can take it off your hands and give you plenty o' money you'd be glad to use.'

'Money, money, money!' she cried. 'I've told you. If you're trying to tell me Sammy Phinn passed a lot of money to my man you're up the wrong close. As a matter of fact many's the time my Hamish lent his brother money, money he never got back.'

'Oh aye, they were thick,' the stranger granted. 'Your man was good to his twin. Sammy told me that himself.'

'Aye, they were twins but quite different,' Mrs Phinn said proudly. 'My Hamish was a good man. He was never the gambler and the drinker and the thief his brother was. It was Sammy broke old Granny Phinn's heart. In and out of jail, in and out of jail.'

'Look, missis,' said the stranger aggrievedly. 'Stop kidding me. You know fine it was Sammy did the Finnieston bank that Thursday.'

Mrs Phinn let out a little scream and her rough hand went to her flat chest and then fluttered to her mouth in alarm. 'Sammy Phinn never did a bank in his life,' she cried. 'He wouldn't dare. Wee sweetie-shops and pubs was his level. A bank! He could no more have did a bank than fly in the air.'

'He did that one all right,' the stranger answered. 'The sweetie shops and the pubs all went to experience, missis. A man's got to learn. He took a year working on it. Got it organized.'

'I don't believe you,' said Mrs Phinn.

'He brought out forty-five thousand pound,' the stranger bashed on, clutching her elbow now though she was too shocked to move. 'He had it in two suitcases and there wasn't more than three quid in his pocket the day he was killed. It's a lot o' money, missis. It canny just have walked.'

'I'm sorry I can't help you,' Mrs Phinn panted. She was frightened. 'I never knew a thing about forty-five thousand pound, I can tell you that. And what's more I don't want to know about it. I'd rather have a clear conscience and my night's sleep than all your money.'

'You keep your conscience and I'll rest content wi' the money,' the stranger bargained. 'The point is I haveny got it. I think you've got it. Sammy had it all in two suitcases when I drove the car away that night. But we couldny stop and divide it at Anderston Cross at two o'clock in the morning, could we? Sammy said we was just to wait till things got quiet. He got out of the car at the Saltmarket and I know he took a taxi your way. I heard him. He went to see Hamish wi' the money. The next thing I hears he's deid and there's nae money on him. Nothing in the bank, nothing in the post-office, nothing in his digs. Missis, this is serious. Hamish must have said something to you.'

'No, I'm afraid you're wrong,' Mrs Phinn told him sincerely. She was beginning to think the man was mad, and she felt less frightened. He could be humoured. 'Hamish never mentioned that kind of money to me, and I can assure you—'

'You're a bloody assurance society, you are!' the stranger interrupted her peevishly. She was sure there was a mad look in his eyes the way he glared at her.

'Yes, I can assure you,' she sailed on, not at all put out by his rudeness. She was used to the way Percy talked to her. 'I can assure you my man wasn't the sort of man to get mixed up in bank robberies. Bank robberies! For goodness sake! Huh-hm!'

She gave one of her special snorts, the violent kind that jarred Percy's nerves.

They glowered at each other, neither yielding, and Mrs Phinn jerked her elbow free from the stranger's clutch.

'Why don't you just go home and go to your bed?' she suggested. 'You've been watching the telly too much.'

'Oh, Jesus Christ!' the stranger cried in pain. He seemed on the point of weeping.

'Now, I don't like blasphemy,' said Mrs Phinn. 'I'm not accustomed to it. If you must swear go and swear somewhere else.'

The stranger stared at her, shaking his head sorrowfully, and she was sure she saw tears glisten in his crafty eyes.

'Missis, are you mad?' he whispered. 'Come on, don't act it! This is serious. I'm only talking to you for your own good. I was just the driver but I'm entitled to my share. I'll play fair wi' you but there's other folk starting to wonder and if they get on to you they'll chiv you as soon as look at you. I'm telling you, missis.'

'I'm sorry, I've got my work to go to,' said Mrs Phinn calmly. 'I told you, I've got to work for my living. We canny all go about robbing banks and living in the lap of luxury. Forty thousand pound! Did ye ever hear the like!'

'Forty-five thousand pound,' the stranger corrected her dourly.

She looked at him pityingly and tutted.

'To a penny?' she asked sarcastically.

'I was talking to your son the other night,' he said abruptly. 'A big fella with splay feet.'

'You can leave my son's feet out of it,' Mrs Phinn objected with dignity. 'He canny help his feet. At least he's no' a wee Glasgow bauchle like you.'

'Aye, all right,' said the stranger huffily. 'I'd rather be a Glasgow bauchle than a big drip like him. Oh, la-de-da. Called after Percy the poet says he. He could do wi' a haircut at that.'

'He never told me,' said Mrs Phinn.

'That's funny,' said the stranger. 'Maybe it's him that knows and he's keeping something back from you.'

'My boy's a big simple soul,' said Mrs Phinn proudly. 'He wouldn't do anything that's wrong. He was never brought up to it.'

'I could see he was kind of dumb,' the stranger agreed neutrally. 'He talks a lot but he doesn't say very much. He's not all that bright I don't think. That's why I never told him what I'm telling you. I wanted to see if he knew anything first. But I don't think he knew a thing.'

'He knows as much as I know then,' said Mrs Phinn.

'Unless he was acting it?' the stranger suggested.

'I can assure you he had nothing to act about,' said Mrs Phinn.

The stranger brooded into Mrs Phinn's thin sour face before he spoke again.

'You see, missis, when Sammy left us at the Saltmarket he told us he'd cellar the money till it was safe to divide it.

Aye, he was the boss. He liked acting the big shot. Wouldny trust us. No' to spend it daft-like right away I mean. No, he'd take care of it. Don't yous worry, he said. Ye can trust me. I'll cellar it safe and sound where it'll never be found. Now what did he mean, cellar it? The only bloke Sammy saw when he left us was your Hamish, and your Hamish has a cellar in the school there, hasn't he?'

'My Hamish is dead,' Mrs Phinn reminded him with a widow's proud sorrow.

'Aye, but the cellar's no',' the stranger commented.

'Yes, the cellar is,' she retorted. She was a contrary woman. She wasn't going to have this layabout telling her about the school cellar. It had been the bane of her husband's last years, it was in such a state, and she wasn't going to have it talked about by any stranger. 'That cellar hasn't been used for twenty years or more. It isn't a cellar at all now, not since they stopped the steam heating.'

'But there's a door there in Tulip Place,' the stranger waved a hand. 'That's the door to the cellar, i'n't it?'

'That door?' said Mrs Phinn, sneering at his mistake. 'That door's blind. There's a brick wall behind it. Has been since the school went all electrical. That's where they delivered the coal in the old days.'

She didn't know her contrary mixture of fact and fiction was a repeat of Percy's story to the stranger, and she didn't understand why he seemed to sag and surrender. She supposed his early morning fit of madness was leaving him.

'Ach well, I can only keep on trying,' he muttered, fishing out a cigarette end from his pocket and lighting it with his head to one side and his lips pouting. 'I'd ha' been on to it sooner only I had to go to Manchester for thirty days.'

'Oh, I see,' she said sympathetically.

In the local idiom 'to go to Manchester' meant to go to jail. She knew that. Her husband had often told her of children who told their teacher their father couldn't sign a form for free meals or free clothes because he was in Manchester. The locution saved everyone embarrassment.

'What did they get you for?' she asked softly, just to let him see she knew the language.

'Loitering with intent. You see, a man like me. A known character. Wan o' Sammy's crowd. But the crowd's no' the same now. We miss Sammy. He put it on a bit but he'd got something. There's no denying it. He took a year rehearsing the Finnieston job, his first real big job. He had a great future, so he had, the same man. Then he had to go and get killed, the stupid bastard. But he had something, oh aye, he had something!'

He smoked and looked over bitterly at the grim three-storeyed school.

'Forty-five thousand pound, that's what he had,' he muttered. 'It canny just have went up in smoke.'

'Come on, Mrs Phinn! You're late!' a voice called through the mild morning air. The janitor was at the front gate, blithe and debonair. Without his hat on, Mrs Phinn noted disapprovingly.

'I'm just coming,' she sang out sedately.

'You can see your boyfriend when you've done your morning's work,' the janitor shouted over to her jovially.

Mrs Phinn glared at him, the stranger scuttled swiftly, and the pigeons on the roof quarrelled noisily. It was a lovely morning. She went into the school, took off her coat, tied a scarf round her head, and started to tackle the classrooms on the top flat.

She saw Percy at tea-time. He came ambling in, splay-footed as usual, round-shouldered to keep his head clear of the ceiling, and looked remarkably untired for a youth who claimed to be doing a hard day's work every day. He sat playing with an Alsatian pup he had bought after he bought his motor-bike. He told his mother it was a stray that had followed him home, and she kept on looking at the small ads in the evening paper in case the owner advertised. There might be a reward for returning it.

'Even ten bob,' she said. 'It's always something.'

'Ten bob!' Percy smiled cunningly. He had paid fifteen pounds for the pup. It had a pedigree. More than I have, he thought bitterly when the dealer told him, and he felt it was another injustice.

'Who would pay ten bob for a wee thing like this?'

He chuckled at his private joke.

'Aye, you bring it here but it's me that's got to feed it and look after it,' his mother complained. 'It's me that's got to take it out for a walk every morning when you're no' here and I could be having a lie-down on my bed. I'm up before six every morning, don't you forget.'

'You don't give me much of a chance to forget it,' he muttered, pretending to throttle the lively pup. He called it Boatswain.

'That's a daft name for a dug,' said his mother. 'What does that mean? Boatswain! Did ye ever hear the likes!'

'That was the name Lord Byron gave his dog,' he told her from the chair. He liked giving information from his chair. It made him feel professorial. 'But you wouldn't know that, would you? I don't suppose you've never heard of Lord George Gordon Byron. You never think of reading poetry, do you? You've never lived, that's your trouble. Me, I've read them all, Shelley and Byron and – and – and eh Keats, and I've read Shakespeare, so I have, and I've read—'

'I have so heard of Lord George Gordon,' his mother cut in, angry with him, before he could think of another poet he had read. 'I seen him in the telly last winter. He was in a serial. It was about folk breaking into prison.'

'Breaking into prison!' he sneered. 'You break out of prison, you don't break in.'

'These folk broke in,' she insisted. 'Lord George Gordon was in it. He was against the Pope. So was your father, in case you forget. You see I have so heard of Lord George Gordon. I'm not as stupid as you like to think. I seen the serial I'm telling you.'

'What serial was that?' he challenged her rudely. 'Lord Byron was never on the telly. He never gave a damn for the Pope.'

'That's what I'm telling you,' his mother answered.

'Just tell me the name of it,' he nagged at her. 'Tell me

what it was called, go on, tell me. You don't know what you're talking about.'

'Barnacle Rudge,' his mother decided after a few moment's brooding over the frying-pan on the gas-ring. She was frying a couple of eggs, and she had some chips in deep fat, for Percy's meal.

'Never heard of it,' said Percy and rolled the pup over, bent forward from his chair.

'I missed bits of it,' his mother admitted. 'Maybe I couldny tell you the story right but I know what it was called. I know what I seen.'

'You couldny follow a serial,' he taunted her. 'You'd never remember what happened the week before. Sure you canny even remember when it's the day for my laundry. You'd have me looking like a tramp if I didn't remind you.'

'Huh-hm, your laundry!' she snorted, and Percy frowned and fidgeted. 'I wish that was all I had to worry me, your laundry.'

Percy had the pup on its back and he ·throttled it lovingly.

His mother simmered. She could keep it in no longer. They were seldom very cordial and they were never given to confiding in each other, but his manner annoyed her, she didn't like dogs, and she wanted to take the conversation off her failings and give it another direction.

'A funny thing happened to me this morning,' she started.

'Ha-ha!' Percy gave a staccato imitation of a ham-actor's laugh.

His mother clenched her teeth, counted ten and went on.

'A man stopped me at the corner of Bethel Street and Tulip Place.'

Percy's large hand loosened its grip on the Alsatian's throat.

'A man?' he said throatily, and he felt his stomach turning over.

'A wee bauchle,' she said, spooning fat over the eggs. 'Wearing a dirty coat. I don't know what he wanted a coat for, a lovely morning like it was this morning. Looked as if he slept in it. To hide his rags I suppose. A right Glasgow ned.'

Percy gaped up at her. His thick underlip hung even lower than usual and the neglected pup squirmed on the carpet beside the empty fireplace and barked for attention.

'He was trying to tell me it was your Uncle Sammy done the Finnieston bank,' she said, and snorted again. 'You remember the Finnieston bank? They still haveny got who done it.'

'Uncle Sammy never done a bank in his life,' Percy objected indignantly. 'He never done anything bigger than McIlweeny's pub and he was caught coming out. Him? He couldny do a bank. He hasny the brains.'

'That's what I told him,' said his mother, turning to the pot with the chips. 'And he says your uncle gave the money to your father to keep for him, and then your uncle was killed in that smash on the Edinburgh road, and your poor father collapsed in the cellar the day after that. Ach, the man was stark raving mad!'

Percy tickled the pup again, his head down.

'You never told me he'd been speaking to you too,' his mother threw at him sharply over her shoulder as she drained the chips in a wire basket.

'Him? Speaking to me?' Percy said as if he was puzzled. 'Och aye, I remember. There was a man stopped me one night in Tulip Place and talked a lot of tommy-rot about the cellar. I sent him away. I wouldny waste time talking to a man like that.'

'He asked me about the cellar too,' said his mother. 'I just told him it was never used at all now. That cellar broke your father's heart. I'm sure that's what drove him to an early death. A man in his forties to die like that, hinging ower a big box o' rubbish. He couldny get that place straight. I don't care what they say. He never had heart trouble when he worked in Sybie Street school. It was the sight of that cellar. He couldny do a thing with it. I just told him the door in Tulip Place was bricked up. I'm no' going to have the likes of him quizzing me about the place where your poor father took a shock and died. He must have lay there for hours before we found him.'

'That's what I told him too,' said Percy.

'Come on, your tea's out,' said his mother, and Percy went to the table followed by his pup. He settled it masterfully at his feet and tossed it the crust of his bread. He didn't eat his crusts.

His brain worked so slowly that for a long time after it had received disturbing information his face remained stolid, slightly vacuous with its thick under-lip hanging loosely. His mother had no inkling he was frightened. He bent his head over the plate, stuffing his face quickly, but all the time his head was throbbing painfully in confusion and dismay. Forking his chips greedily in threes and fours he comforted himself. The stranger was a bird of ill-omen, that was sure. But he had no right to the money. Nobody had any right to the money. Nobody but the person who had a right to the place where it was found. It was nobody's money, so it was his. Uncle Sammy could never have had anything to do with such countless wealth. Uncle Sammy? Uncle Sammy was a fly man that couldn't keep out of jail. He could never have been the goose that laid the golden egg. No, no, a thousand times no! Ah, sweet mystery of life, and this was a mystery too. Poetry dealt with mysteries and so did poets, and he was a poet. He was still the chosen of El. And he had been very fair dividing it amongst the under-privileged children who hadn't a decent pair of shoes to their name. It had been given to him for a purpose. He had been true to the purpose revealed to him. He would give in to nobody. Nobody would frighten him. His stupid mother and the bauchly stranger wanted to bring the money back down to earth and explain it. But it didn't belong there. It wasn't to be explained as easily as that. It came from heaven. You had to have faith.

He gobbled his egg and chips in a flurry of fear and washed at the kitchen sink.

'I've got nervous dyspepsia, that's what I've got,' he

thought into the towel as he dried his face. 'It's an awful responsibility to carry. But you've got to face your destiny. I'll see it through, so I will.'

'Are you not shaving the night?' his mother asked slyly. 'You usually shave before you go out after your tea. What's up? Are you no' seeing her the night?'

'I'm not seeing anybody,' he answered, quelling her with a look. Her question reminded him of Sophy, and that was an offence.

'Where are you going then?' his mother asked.

'Out,' he informed her concisely.

'Ach, I bet you're going to meet some girl! I don't know what a fellow your age is bothering about girls at all for. You're far too young, and without a penny in your pocket. I don't know how you do it.'

He let that go. He wouldn't boast about what he had in his pocket. The elect don't boast they've been chosen. As for girls, he wanted to forget them after last night. He was beginning to remember that once he had wanted nothing but peace, peace and quiet.

'Funny how you get too busy to do what you meant to do,' he thought, pleased at his understanding of human nature.

But now it was high time to make sure he found peace. Sophy had let him down and the stranger was getting too near. He was heart-sick and disgusted at seeing wealth passed to outsiders in defiance of the oath to El, he was bitter at the way the Brotherhood had abandoned the religion he had tried to teach them. It was time to go away.

He walked round the town, a slim torch in his hip-pocket, loitered in the Central Station, felt himself superior to the humanity oozing around him there, and when it was getting dark he went back to Bethel Street. He slouched up and down Tulip Place for quarter of an hour till he was sure there were no watching eyes in the blind-alley and slipped into the cellar.

CHAPTER TWELVE

Earlier that night Helen Garson was waiting across the street from the garage where her man worked. She was there before five o'clock, still wearing her uniform. But she was on an early shift, and finished for the day. She preferred to watch and wait till her man came out rather than go home and change and call at his house. She had long persuaded herself she would never go back there. He came out fifteen minutes late.

'That's him all right,' she recognized disapprovingly. 'Never could stop sharp. Many a good meal he wasted. Unpaid overtime, that's what he does, but you can't tell him anything.'

She beckoned discreetly with one arm up and a slight side-to-side movement of her hand, a royal admission that she was there to be seen and welcomed. Bob Garson was aware at once of the green uniform across the street. Every time he saw a bus conductress he was reminded of his wife, and he would have kept his head down and passed on, burying the memory as he always did when he saw one, but the little wave of the hand halted him in a twilight of two minds at the graveside. He looked, he saw, he recognized. You would never have believed a man could be so embarrassed at being stopped in the street by his own wife. After all, he had courted her, he had married her, he had slept with her, he had begotten a child on her, he had seen her in her underwear and less, and now he was blushing and awkward at the sight of her on the Queen's highway in the hardly glamorous coat and skirt of a female employee of Glasgow Corporation Transport. But she was that kind of woman. It didn't matter what she wore. She was always herself, a rare womanly presence. He stood on one side of the street and she stood on the other. It was where they had left off: a test of wills. She waited and he waited. She beckoned again, with the index finger of her right hand crooked and signalling. For all the silence of her summons it might as well have been the song the sirens sang. She won. He crossed over. Yes, he was scowling, he was quite unamiable, he hadn't a word to throw at her in greeting, his heart was black and his face was red, but though he was no Caesar he had crossed his Rubicon. But he didn't know that when he made a brewer's lorry stop at the pedestrian crossing to let him over.

'What's Frank been up to?' she asked coldly.

'I don't know what you're talking about,' he answered, iceberg to iceberg, but of course we are told by those who know that kind of thing that two-thirds of an iceberg lie below the surface.

'That's a fine one!' she cried indignantly. 'You ask me to come home because of Frank and then you try to tell me you don't know what he's been doing. Well, I'm telling you straight, I'm not coming back home. I mean I'm not coming back to your house, till I know what it's all about.'

'What what's all about?' he looked at her strong wilful face with a grudge. But he couldn't hold her eyes, and he looked down. That was no better. Even in that thick coat and graceless skirt she looked well. He knew she had a good figure, and he resented that too.

'You tell me,' she said boldly. 'It was you that started it.'

'It was you that started it,' he echoed her. 'You left me of your own free will and as far as I'm concerned you can stay away.'

'So that's your story now, is it?' she nodded wisely. 'You want me to crawl, do you? I'll see you in hell first. You think because you put a bit in the paper I'm going to come running back to you? Aye! Come back, all is forgiven! Who do you think you are to start forgiving anybody? You're going to forgive me, are you? So I've to admit I was in the wrong! Oh no, Bob! Oh, no!'

Her thoughtless use of his name tingled him, puzzled him, confused him.

'What are you trying to do?' he asked, bewildered. 'What

are you talking about, a bit in the paper? You think you can kid me, do you? You think I'm still—'

He stopped and scowled at her. He had come too near saying part of their trouble, that she had ruled him because he so much wanted her that he always had to have her. It was his way of solving all differences. But it wasn't hers. She wanted to win arguments by withholding herself. At that point, hating her for playing on his weakness and even despising his weakness, he denied himself, denied her, and told her to come into the house for good or leave it for good.

'You'd cut off your nose to spite your face,' she told him when he took that position. 'You'd rather do without me altogether than let me go out to work.'

'It's not a question of my nose and my face,' he had shouted at her that last night. 'It's a question of who's boss in this house. If you think because I—'

He stopped then as he stopped now. He wouldn't say it, he wouldn't admit it. She was taking what he called an unfair advantage, standing there so straight and confident, so well-made and womanly even in that uniform he hated.

'It's you that's trying to kid me,' she threw back at him in anger. She always was a spitfire. 'If you didn't want me back why did you go to all that trouble of putting it in the paper?'

His healthy honest face, almost stupid in its bewilderment, made her throw out an explosive sigh of exasperation. She fumbled inside her tunic at her right breast while he watched her hand with sad memoried eyes, and shoved the newspaper cutting across to him. He took it and read it. He read it twice, and he was still out of his depth.

'I never put that in,' he frowned. 'I don't know anything about it. Frank was in a fight a couple of days ago and I thought that's what you were talking about. He was all kicks and bruises. Because of you.'

'How because of me?' she demanded, straighter than ever. 'I haven't even seen the kid for four years.'

'Well, you know whose fault that is,' he charged her.

'Yes, yours,' she countered immediately.

He preferred not to answer that.

'One of the boys in his class said you ran away with a darkie,' he chose to answer instead. 'And he thought he had to stand up for you. But he got the worst of it. That was all.'

She laughed and cried all at once.

'A darkie!' she said, nearly hysterical. 'Oh God! I wish that was all that was to it. I've lived without a man for four years.'

'I wish I could believe that,' he muttered sourly.

'That's your trouble,' she spat fire at him again. 'You've got a bad mind. You liked to kid on you just had to be head of the house and I should stay at home, but there was more than that to it. You didn't trust me. You were jealous. You liked to think that every man I worked with was making love to me. Why can't you grow up? The world's not like that at all. The men I worked with had their wives and family and they were perfectly happy. They liked me and I liked them and that's all there was to it. But not for you, oh no! You had to make more of it because you've got a bad mind. You wouldn't trust me, that was your real trouble. Oh, I saw through you all right!'

'You should have said that long ago,' he defended himself weakly. 'I would have trusted you if you had only told me you didn't want another man.'

'I shouldn't have needed to tell you if you had sense at all,' she answered impatiently. 'I married you, didn't I? Who else would I want? I'm not a filmstar, I'm a girl from Fife. When I marry, I'm stuck with the man I married. I know all your faults and I've no doubt you know mine. You told me them often enough. But I never looked for a man since the day I left you. I never left you because I was bothered about a man. That's got nothing to do with it and you know it. But you like to kid yourself.'

'Oh, but Helen!' he muttered, so embarrassed by her bluntness that he evaded it. 'That boy took a terrible beating. I saw his side. He was kicked, Helen, he was kicked something shocking. Standing up for you.'

'That's got nothing to do with it,' she brought him back to the issue. She jabbed her finger on the cutting he was still holding. 'That got your name.'

'Aye, but it's not mine,' he said, quite firm with her on that point. 'I never asked you to come home. I never put that in the paper.'

'Then it was Frank,' she said quickly. 'What does he mean? He's got loads. Is that a disease, or has he won the pools?'

'Don't be daft,' he retorted impulsively. 'A boy of ten wouldn't know how to fill in a coupon.'

'Well, what does it mean?' she insisted.

'How should I know?' he countered in the traditional Scots way, answering one question by another.

They stood in the broad evening sun, arguing like any husband and wife where the wife has a perfectly good point that the man can't answer, and the woman keeps at it and the man tells her she is talking nonsense, and they didn't see till later that they were on speaking terms again. So long as you keep quarrelling you're still speaking. Their argument brought them together on the normal terms of married life, and it was a long time since either of them had been so worked up about anything.

'It's Frank,' said Mrs Garson. 'I'm sure it's Frank. It was Frank I'm telling you. It was him put it in the paper.'

'Don't talk soft,' said Mr Garson superiorly. 'How could it be Frank? Where would he get the money to pay for putting adverts in a paper? Damnit, he couldn't even write an advert, he's only ten.'

'Aye, but he's a clever boy,' his mother claimed. 'At least he was, unless you've knocked him stupid. He took after the Grahams, no' the Garsons.'

'The Grahams!' Mr Garson despised them with his tone. 'Like your big sister Nessie that could hardly read or write. The postcard she sent us from Saltcoats. We've had no rain. Kay-enn-oh-double-you. Oh aye, she was a rare scholar!'

'Maybe she didn't spell so good,' Mrs Garson admitted.

'But she made a damn good job of that wee paper shop she got out of the compen-money when her man was killed at his work.'

'Aye, she did all right. And she never thought of coming to see her nephew, not once. She couldn't even send him a Christmas card.'

'What do you expect? And since when were you ever bothered about Christmas?'

'She could have sent him some wee thing, the boy's got nothing.'

'You put me out the house and then you think my big sister's going to run after you and your boy! You've got some rare ideas you have. You'd make a cat laugh you would!'

'Your boy,' Mr Garson cut in before she finished.

'He's yours too,' said Mrs Garson. 'Or is that something else you don't trust me for?'

'I never said that,' he answered, shocked at her. 'But if you're going to suggest things—'

'There see what I mean?' she appealed to him against himself. 'A wee bit sarcasm and you canny take it. You start thinking things. You must have an awful life with a mind like yours!'

'With a wife like you,' he answered dourly.

'I've told you all I'm going to tell you,' she said sharply. 'I told you I married you and that's enough for me. If you can't make sense of that and see what I'm telling you then you're even thicker than I thought you were.'

'Well, would you come back?' he asked. He knew quite well what she was telling him, but he liked making himself sour and suspecting her of all kinds of duplicities.

'Would I come back?' she echoed him in a voice of over-acted astonishment. 'You're after arguing you never asked me. You're after telling me to stay away for good.'

'Because of the way you approached me,' he said defensively.

'You're getting away from the point,' she stalled. 'There's that thing I tore out of the paper. If that wasn't Frank who

136

was it. I want to see him. You've kept him from me long enough. I want to see him.'

'Now?' he nearly shouted, as if the idea was outrageous.

'Well, I don't mean next Christmas,' she snapped at him.

They moved off together, hardly hand in hand, but both at peace, quite reconciled. After all, they were both Scots. There is nothing puzzles the Scot more than the Englishman's claim not to wear his heart on his sleeve. To a Scotsman, the Englishman wears his heart like a breast-pocket handkerchief, stuck in front of him for show, and flaunts it in public too. To the Garsons, their crabbit conversation had been a warming bout of making love, and their final snarl at each other had given them all the confidence of the final kiss that knows it isn't final because the best is yet to be.

The only thing that still bothered them was the small ad in the *Citizen*. They were straining at the leash to get home and see Frank and sort the whole thing out.

'Damn cheek, putting our names in the papers,' muttered Mr Garson. 'Anybody might have seen it.'

'He was doing it for the best,' said Mrs Garson. 'He was always a sensitive boy.'

'You never thought of that when you left him without a mother's care,' said Mr Garson.

'You never thought of that when you wouldn't let me see him unless I gave in to you.'

'You didn't make much of an effort.'

'Ach, my mother died when I was eight, and I lived,' Mrs Garson remembered callously.

And chatting in that way, with true Scots friendliness, they walked the short distance from the garage in Bethel Street to the tenement where Frank was making tea, twenty-seven Ossian Street, three-up the far-away.

The boy was frying sliced sausages and eggs for his father's tea, and he was hot-headed with anxiety as he stood at the gas-cooker in a corner of the kitchen. He had begun his evening routine at the usual time, right after he finished his paper-rake, but his father was late. He didn't know what to do for the best. If he took the frying-pan off the gas his father would walk in when the sausages were cold and the eggs sloppy. And if he kept the frying-pan on the gas the sausages would get charred and hard and the eggs would get all brown and burnt round the edges, and that would be when his father would walk in. It was the way of the world. You couldn't win.

He tried a compromise. He held the pan above the blue flames of the gas-ring and kept moving the sausages and eggs round and round in the pan so that at least they wouldn't stick to the bottom. He was doing all right, quite engrossed in his compromise as an end itself, a task with its own interest, watching the sizzling fat and the changing colour of the sausages, when the kettle on the other ring came to the boil. The lid moved in the angry, turbulent way that attracted the attention of James Watt as early as 1759, though it isn't generally known that he had been anticipated by Robert Hooke, but Frank Garson was no Watt. He was only a ten-year-old schoolboy in a panic, trying to prepare the evening meal for his father in a motherless, wifeless house. He slapped the frying-pan down on the gas-ring again and lowered the gas under the kettle. Another problem reared its ugly head. If he brewed the tea at once it would probably be too strong by the time his father came in. If he didn't brew it the water would inevitably be off the boil altogether before his father came in. The real trouble was his father didn't like to be kept waiting. He was a just man according to himself, but an impatient one according to those who knew him. The sweat on the boy's brow glided down his nose and down behind his ears. It wasn't just his anxiety nor even the heat from the cooker. The summer evening was still hot, and the kitchens in the tall tenements were all stifling airless boxes of irritating heat.

He was coping with a simmering kettle and a sizzling frying-pan, willing to be happy enough with either if only the other weren't there, when his father and mother walked in on him. His father never knocked or rang. He always had his key. That was what seemed to make his entrances so abrupt.

'Oh my godfather! Are you still using that thing?' the boy's mother cried at once. She deliberately ignored her son and crossed to the old gas-cooker, tutting at it as she took charge. She wouldn't let any man see that the sight of her only child moved her at all. But the cooking facilities were a subject of comment and attention.

'It was you that bought it,' her husband reminded her dourly.

'Aye, eleven years ago,' she retorted. 'Things has changed a bit since then or haven't you heard? Holy Christmas, even my landlady's all-electric.'

She brewed the tea deftly, soothed the misunderstood sausages and eggs, elevated them with a flip of a fish-lifter, served them skilfully on a couple of plates, and kept nagging her man.

'You've no idea, Bob! You're content to live like your grandfather. You've never heard of the wind of change blowing through the kitchens of Britain. I was always surprised that a man like you, so clever with cars and bang-up-to-date on models, and you just never bothered your backside what women can get nowadays.'

'Frank, here's your mother come to see you,' Mr Garson answered, very stiff, annoyed at his wife's reference to cars. He had no car, nor was like to have one, but he could tell the make and model of any car a hundred yards away, and it was hardly a thing to be sneered at if he could take a motor-engine apart and reassemble it. He knew his job, that was all. But fridges and tellies were a piece of nonsense.

The boy hovered a little distance from the conquered gas-cooker. If this was his mother then that grimy contraption was no longer his concern. He had no wish to defend his claim to it. But he was shy when his father spoke to him. This woman in the green uniform of a Corporation bus-conductress wasn't so much his mother as a person like someone he remembered, a long long time ago.

As if to introduce herself his mother ruffled his thick

139

waving crop of chestnut-brown hair, a gesture of affection not unlike the spasm that had seized Noddy's mother when she came home with the two ten-shilling notes she had wheedled out of old Daunders. Like Noddy, Frank Garson jerked his head away, distressed. Yet his scalp tingled, and he wondered what to do to reach her.

The three of them sat at the table in a silence as solid as the walls of Edinburgh Castle. The head of the house was hungry and he wolfed in, but he tried to break through by asking his wife to have something to eat.

'No, I'm all right,' she said calmly. 'A cup of tea's all I want.'

She had taken off her coat and her blouse was smart, her ungracious green skirt with the thin red stripe hidden as she sat at the table between her husband and her son. The latter squinted at her as he ate. He was too young to have nervous indigestion, but the state he was in wasn't likely to do his digestion any good. His heart was going so emphatically he was sure it must sound like the alarm clock in the other room, his middle was the site of a civil war, and his palate was as parched as if he was a man with a hangover. He kept on squinting because he liked the look of this strange woman. Before he has the possibility of a sexual appreciation even a boy of ten has an aesthetic appreciation of a woman, and Frank Garson warmed to his mother. This was no sour dame with specs and a flat front like Percy's blighted mother, this was a woman like the kind you saw in photographs in the papers. This was like the woman he had dreamed he had kissed when he was in Miss Montgomery's class, a woman that was at one and the same time Miss Montgomery and wasn't. Not once but three times, and the dreams puzzled him when they came back to him the next day, recalled by a word, a sight, a sound. He had left his seat in class, walked out and kissed Miss Montgomery, only of course it wasn't Miss Montgomery, it was somebody else who was Miss Montgomery. But what had he to do with kissing? The memory of the three dreams allured and repelled him. He felt he had been brave, he felt he had been ridiculous. What would his classmates have said if he had told any of them he had dreamt he had kissed Miss Montgomery? But not of course Miss Montgomery, because she was really Mrs Joyce and her husband was a captain in the Merchant Navy and she was a fit wife for a ship's commander, so well dressed and beautiful. Had he been ridiculous or just gallant? It baffled him, and although it was only yesterday he had been Miss Montgomery's lover it was also a thousand years ago, another world, another person.

'Take your time,' said his mother. 'You're shoving that down your throat as if you hadn't seen food for a week. You're not chewing it at all.'

He put his eyes on his plate and he chewed.

'And another thing,' said his mother. 'You've got some explaining to do, young man.'

It was only with those words that he remembered the silly advert he had put in the *Citizen*. He had made up that advert in a mood, much as a man might utter an oath in privacy, and no more than that man had he expected to find his words having any influence on the real world he couldn't escape from. He was frightened. The civil war in his middle was settled by a truce that merely raised new problems. His heart slowed. His brain left its confusion of his mother with Miss Montgomery and settled on a simplified memory of Percy. He would be better to say nothing. His mother was back and he was sure she wouldn't go away again in a hurry. He didn't need to say anything to keep her. He had an old loyalty now to remember. He would admit the advert and pretend it was only a trick to get her to come back.

That's what he thought. But when his mother slapped the newspaper cutting on the table in front of him he saw he wasn't going to be coaxed to admit it was his work. He was being told. He heard the rumbling of approaching disaster. He felt very small and unready. He had a passing memory of the time he had tried to pick up a full-size football with one hand. It was far too big for his grasp, he had to let it drop. And so it was now. He would have to let go.

Yet even in the rout of his plans he noticed it was his mother leading the attack. His father just sat there and glowered.

'Your face gives you away,' his mother said sternly, and he felt his face hot with the blush of known guilt. 'It was you, wasn't it?'

She pretended to be asking him but he knew she was telling him. He nodded, afraid that if he spoke he would start crying, and he wasn't going to cry in front of any woman, especially not this one.

'What do you mean, loads?' his mother demanded, her finger jabbing three times at the simple word, her other elbow on the table, her face close against him, intimidating him.

'A li-li-lot,' he answered with difficulty. He always had trouble with his 'l's, his throat was all tightened with anxiety, and people who frightened him always brought upon him the fear that his erratic stammer would win and make him ridiculous.

'What do you mean a lot?' his mother persisted. Her face was so close now, she was staring at him so hard as if she was trying to hypnotize him, that he was drowned in the dark-brown depths of her eyes, and a wisp of her hair touched his brow. But though her eyes and hair were soft her voice was hard. 'When did you get a lot? Where? Have you been doing the pools?'

He smiled unsurely, then he saw she wasn't being funny at all. She was still grim. She really meant it. He wiped the smile off his face with a jolted reflex and shook his head.

'Where did you get the money to pay for putting an advert in the papers?' his father asked suddenly.

'Out my tips,' he said quickly, glad for a question he could answer reasonably.

'Not out of the loads of money you say you've got?' his mother suggested, and he wilted under the dry irony of her tone.

'No, I – I – I haven't got loads,' he admitted in crumpled misery.

'Then why did you say loads?'

His mother kept at him, and he suffered for a moment a strange fear that she wanted to be told he really had loads of money so that she could claim her share right away as his mother. Then he saw it was his fault, not hers, if that's how it was. He had hinted at money to get her back. So why should he be disappointed if she came back and asked for some? It was only what he had planned. He hung his head in shame at his own muddle. His plan had been a mistake from the start, and he learnt then that to use certain ways of getting what we want means that what we wanted wasn't worth having. But he wouldn't believe that of his mother.

'Why did you say loads?' she was repeating, hammering at him.

She grabbed him by the hair and shook his head to make him look up and answer her.

He broke. This woman blasted his loyalty to Percy. His loyalty to the Brotherhood he knew was already withered. He had never heard of *la femme fatale*, all he knew was that this woman was ruling him, that he felt himself an inferior part of her, and had to give in to her, because the whole is greater than the part. He wept a little and came out with his story through little sobs. It had to come out. He was sick with keeping it in. Maybe now he could sleep at night without bad dreams and take his dinner with some pleasure in what he was eating. It was like putting down a heavy load he had been carrying too far without a rest.

'I haven't got loads but I know where there is loads because it was me that found it in the cellar, in the cellar in the school. I said we ought to tell the police and I thought Percy would agree but he didn't, and he's giving it out to the gang every week but I wouldn't take any. Everybody was getting money so I thought why shouldn't I get a share because it was me that found it, but I didn't want it for myself like them, they've been spending it on rubbish and things they can't use, but I could take hundreds for you if it's money you want. You went away to get money, so if it's money you want I can get you hundreds, or thousands if you like. I can get it if you want it, cause I know there's still loads left in spite of Percy. I know. I've seen it. But I don't like it. I still think the police ought to be told. You don't know what's behind it.'

He stopped. He couldn't speak any more. His sobs and his stammer beat him.

The husband and wife looked at each other anxiously, each seeming to expect the other to have the solution.

'Has he been keeping all right?' Mrs Garson whispered across the table, her clutch on her son's thick hair slackening to an absent-minded caress of his skull.

'There's never been a thing wrong with him since you went away,' Mr Garson answered aggressively, provoked at the insinuation that the boy was mad and he didn't know it.

Mrs Garson put one hand across her son's forehead. It was fevered all right, but hardly the fever of delirium. She was a woman, she was an intelligent woman. She had intuition. She could recognize when the truth was passing by, whatever odd garment it was wearing at the moment. She kept at the broken boy, determined to make him whole again. His life was more important to her than her own. She was only the tree. The fruit was more important. She couldn't be at peace till she had made sense of him. She nagged at him, patiently, kindly though sometimes a little harshly, but always bearing down firmly on the issue. Her husband sat admiring her with a silent grudge. He could never have done what she was doing, but he saw she was right. She kept at the boy. She bullied him, she loved him, she smacked him, she caressed him. She was a good mother to him. She went over and over his story with him, sobering him with her careful questions. Even Mr Daunders could have learnt something of the art of interrogation from her. She even got out of him the story of how Savage had picked on him for not taking a share of the money and then dragged her name into it before the fight that turned out to be a massacre.

'So there's the fight you were trying to tell me about,' she said indignantly to her husband. 'You didn't dig very deep, did you?'

'Well, damn it all,' he retorted, just as indignant as she was. 'Boys are always fighting. How was I to know there was—'

He searched his boyhood for a cutting phrase.

'Buried treasure!' he finished sarcastically.

'There's no use talking like that,' she turned on him. 'I think you should take him round and see the police.'

'I'm not going near the police, I can tell you that,' her man answered quickly. 'I'll go to the school with him tomorrow morning if you like. I don't mind seeing old Daunders. I've met him before, he's all right, but I'm not going to no police.'

He fiddled with his knife and fork across his dirty plate.

'Thousands and thousands,' he muttered. 'I'd like to see it.'

There was silence except for the boy's diminishing sobs.

'Stop snuffling and redd the table,' said his father abruptly. 'Come away ben, Helen, I want to talk to you.'

The routine job soothed the boy's nerves and he put a kettle on the gas to get hot water for the dishes. It was good to be alone again, and he felt strangely happy at the way he had been left alone. He could hear a murmuring of earnest conversation in the other room, the clish-clash of two people disputing but not on bad terms. At least they weren't quarrelling.

He was drying the knives when his father called him. His parents were standing close together in the lobby between the two rooms, behind the half-open front door.

'Your mother's going away now,' said his father. 'Say goodbye to her.'

He looked up at her and said nothing. She clutched his hair and shook his head again.

'It's time you were getting a haircut,' she said. 'You might have pinched the price of a haircut out your cellar instead of cheating the barber. Well, I'll be seeing you.'

'Go and get your dishes done,' his father muttered and pushed him back into the kitchen.

'I've done the dishes,' he answered, grudging the way he was dismissed, but he had to go, with that strong hand thrusting him.

Yet as he returned to the sink he was aware over his shoulder that his parents were still standing there together. He had a quick glimpse of them coming together in a swift hug and he knew they were kissing.

'Will she be coming back?' he risked later in the evening, an impulse letting him say what an hour's brooding hadn't given him the courage to say.

'Who's she?' his father asked primly.

'M-my m-mother,' he took the rebuke nervously. Sometimes the 'm's were as unpredictable as the 'l's.

'Well, you don't just call your mother she. You speak of her with some respect. You say my mother, you don't refer to her as she.'

His father rested a moment after the strain of that lecture on etiquette. Then he answered the question.

'Of course she'll be coming back. But not tonight. These things take time. She's got – I mean your mother's got to settle things up where she's living. But you'll see her at the end of the week. It'll be all right, don't you worry. Now about this story of yours, you've got to come with me tomorrow and we'll see your headmaster and we'll go into it and—'

His father blethered on, but he wasn't listening. The money seemed of no importance. He was glad it was out of his hands.

'Your mother'll be there too,' his father was saying. 'She can speak better than I can. She's good at explaining things. You know, your mother could talk the hind leg off a donkey once she gets started.'

'Will she be staying here, I mean will my mother be staying here?' the boy felt bold enough to ask. He was amazed at the difference in his father. He had never seen him so light and cheery. He remembered an encyclopedia he had seen in the school library. It showed the mammoths that once roamed over Europe before the coming of the Ice Age, and then it had drawings showing the retreat of the Ice Age. His father, once so huge and cold, now seemed a new and smaller continent, a Europe after an ice age.

'Well, maybe not here,' said the altered man. 'I was just telling your mother. They're building an awful lot of petrol stations the now on all the main roads out of the city. You know away up between Springburn and Bishopbriggs, aye and on to Kirkintilloch? There's nothing but petrol stations on both sides of the road. Well, I know one of them, but it's not out that way, it's more the Stepps direction, and it's actually got a house above the station. How would you like to live in a place like that? You see, this place never suited your mother. It was far too small, and she couldn't be doing with buildings all round her. Your mother was born in the country. She wouldn't mind living out in the wilderness again. And then you see she'd have space for the kind of things she wants. I can get that job there with the house above it, with two bedrooms too, mind you, I can get it if I want it. There's nothing I don't know about cars. I could manage a place like that with my eyes shut. Anybody would do for the pumps, but what they want is a man that would know what to do in an emergency, a manager. That's me.'

He had never heard his father boast before. He listened, fascinated. But he wasn't so much concerned with his father's ability to cope with a service and filling-station as with the prospect of escape. If he had to go to the police, if he had to tell old Daundy all about the cellar, it didn't matter any more. Once it would have frightened him, but not now. Once he would have feared the vengeance of the Brotherhood, but now he could leave the Brotherhood behind him just as easily as he had stopped reading the *Beano*. As for Percy, he found he had no feeling. Yesterday he would have died for him. Today, he wouldn't cross the street to speak to him. So sudden is the death of a boy's love. And his mother would be there. He hadn't felt the least bit jealous when he knew his father was hugging and kissing her like a man and woman on television. On the contrary, he was pleased. It made his father a better and surer means of bringing his mother back than all that business about the money. He didn't want to go through with that. Now he was up against the test he had blundered into, he still didn't want to touch the money. He was at peace that they hadn't asked him to get the hundreds and thousands he had said he could get. He could trust them. He would sleep tonight all right.

'Who is this Percy fellow anyway?' his father was asking him.

'Oh, he's a nice big fellow,' the boy answered vaguely. 'But he's a bit up in the clouds most of the time. You see, he's a kind of poet.'

CHAPTER THIRTEEN

'It's a very true saying when you come to think about it,' Percy told himself as he went carefully down the chute, his little torch stabbing the darkness with a long dagger of light. 'Familiarity breeds contempt. They've forgot they ever made a gentlemen's agreement, so they have. They don't even bother to come to the Friday Night Service any more, well, most of them anyway, there was only four there last week counting me, and when they do come they just mumble through it and want to get out quick. They've no respect for anything now. And you can't trust them. I don't trust Savage for one. He's sleekit, that fellow. I wouldn't be surprised if he was getting in somehow and shifting it. Anyway there's some of them getting money behind my back. Well, it doesn't matter to me now, I'm finished with them. I've wasted too much of my time on them already.'

The cellar was eerie with so much throbbing darkness

fighting powerfully against the thin yellow line of his torch, and he shivered a little. But that was his nerves, not the cold. He had never been farther away from his front-close than the banks of Loch Lomond, and now he was set to go to Land's End. It didn't seem possible to go any farther, short of leaving the country altogether – and that would have meant getting a passport, but he couldn't get his own passport till he was twenty-one. So Land's End it had to be.

'My Ultimate Thool,' he called it.

From Land's End he would travel along the coast. He could buy a mo-bike when he got there. When he found a good spot far from anywhere he would buy a little cottage. There must be hundreds of cottages in these lonely parts of England. He would find one where the sun was warm, the sky was clear, and the waves were dancing fast and bright. Then he would settle in and write a play for television. Not for the money. He didn't need money. But it would be great to see the words on the screen: Specially Written for Television by Percy Phinn. That would be one in the eye for old Elginbrod if she was still living, the old bitch. He had thought of a good title too. *Rabbits With Ostrich Feathers*. He liked that. It was striking, puzzling, original. All he had to do was get to Land's End, find a cottage, get peace and quiet, and think up a plot.

He strode like a conqueror to the corner where he had hidden his briefcase, checked his pyjamas and shaving tackle, and advanced boldly on the tea-chests. He pushed the first two aside and attacked the third, the one he had always kept in reserve. First he broke one bundle of twenty fivers and stuffed the notes into his wallet so as to have plenty of money easy to get at on his journey. Then he began to fill the briefcase. It was only when he had stowed away a couple of dozen bundles that it struck him the chest wasn't as full as it ought to be. He was nearly at the bottom already. He stopped, frowned, and brooded.

'Somebody's been here,' he decided cautiously. 'There should be a lot more than this.'

It gave an extra push to his eagerness to pack up and go. Things weren't right. He had felt it for a long time.

He speeded up filling his briefcase. Two thousand five hundred, two thousand six hundred, two thousand seven hundred. And he still had room for as much more. If need be, he would fill up from the other chests. Meanwhile, he went on trying to empty the one he was at. At two thousand nine hundred he heard a rustle. He wasn't sure where it came from. He froze, his hand halted between the chest and the briefcase, a large hand holding a bundle of five-pound notes in an elastic band. He stayed frozen, listening and counting. He had never heard his heart beat before, and the sound frightened him. It didn't seem right that his life should depend on that sound going on and on. He was in a panic, poised between time and eternity. A creak, and then another rustle.

Was it a draught? There was no wind in the cellar, there couldn't be, the summer night was airless. A rat? But there were no rats.

He shoved the bundle of fivers into his case, covered what was left in the chest with handfuls of old clothes and paper chains and pushed the chest back into its corner. Then turning suddenly like a cowboy quick on the draw firing six rounds rapid from his trusty forty-five he raked the cellar with his torch. Bang at one wall, crack at another, swift shots into the corners. His messengers of light swept the cellar clean. They caught something – a foot, a leg. He raised his aim and dazzled the eyes of a familiar face.

'It's you!' he cried, nearly foaming with fury. 'I might have known!'

'Hello, Perse, old boy,' said Savage pleasantly, coming out into the open from the jungle of broken chairs and *Sunshine Readers*, wearing his black jacket and jeans and putting on his comic English accent to disarm his enemy. 'Robbed any good banks lately, me old cock sparra?'

He had a torch too and he flashed it into Percy's eyes, an insolent retaliation that made Percy really mad. Oh, he was angry now all right. He was ripe for murder. Miss Elginbrod wouldn't have been surprised. She would have said it was all in his medical record: enuresis and hysteria in the infant department, treatment at the Child Guidance Clinic for anti-social behaviour when he was in the juniors, proposals to commit to a special school when he was in the seniors. What could you expect, she would have asked. But a youth doesn't need to have a medical history to be capable of murder.

Savage flashed Percy up and down, teasing him. Percy shoved his torch in his pocket and barged at him. He hit him on the wrist with the edge of his palm and Savage's torch clattered to the stone floor.

'You little rat!' he screamed, wrestling with him in darkness. 'You've been stealing the money, that's what you've been doing! You think I don't know!'

'And what were you doing there?' Savage croaked weakly with Percy's claws at his throat. 'Just taking it out to give it an airing?'

He fought back wildly and brought his knee up hard against Percy's crutch. Percy yelped in an extremity of agony and fell on the floor. Savage jumped on him and kept punching him on the nose and mouth. But for all his height and strength he was only a boy trying to fight a young man twice his size. His defeat was only a matter of time.

Percy took the punches woodenly till the sickness brought on by that knee bashed in between his legs left him. He bided his time deliberately. He knew he was bigger and stronger. He heaved Savage off, scrambled up, and while Savage still rolled on the floor he kicked him in the legs, on the ribs, on the arms, and when Savage squirmed over he kicked him hard on the bottom and between his shoulder blades. He was beginning to enjoy it.

'Yuh big bastard!' Savage screamed, sprawled out like a frog.

He wriggled along the floor and got to his feet clear of Percy's size ten shoes with the thick crepe soles.

'I'll get ye for that,' he said, fierce in the darkness,

whipped off his Army webbing-belt and swung it. The brass clasp came viciously down, just missed Percy's face and hit him where his neck joined his shoulder. Percy sagged with a new pain, and now there was hate in the darkness, a lust of hate between them. They were both panting with eagerness for the ultimate violence, as inflamed as two lovers in darkness. Percy rushed in close to get under the range of the flailing belt and Savage wrapped it round his neck and tried to throttle him. Percy groaned, pulled at it, and heaved. Then he used his knee the way Savage had done to him and Savage fell writhing and cursing on top of a fallen column of *Sunshine Readers*, his belt lost, both hands at his crutch. Percy knelt over, clasping him between his thighs and grabbed him by the ears.

'I wasted months ower you, tae try and teach you for tae be decent,' he cried bitterly. 'Months, and months, and months!' He banged Savage's head on the floor.

'But ye had nae idea!'

He banged it twice again, and some *Sunshine Readers* slid under Savage's head.

'Ye're nae use, to anybody!'

He had lathered himself into a fury and went on pulling Savage's skull up by the ears and then bashing it down to the rhythm of his words.

'Savage by name and Savage by nature. You spoiled my gang, you ruined my plans, you'd take the good out a bad egg, so you would, you rotten little bugger. And you've been raiding the money. Admit it, admit it, admit it!'

Savage moaned, and a sound like a death rattle came up from his bared quivering throat. Then he was quiet.

Until then Percy wanted to do what he was doing and he didn't care what happened to Savage. He was living entirely in the present moment, giving Savage no more than Savage had asked for. He was the righteous man punishing wickedness. But the moment Savage stopped struggling and lay silent, he overflowed with regret for what he had done. He was sorry, truly sorry. He slapped Savage's face, a pale flower in the darkness, once on each cheek. There was something almost tender in those two little slaps.

'Come on, stop acting it,' he said severely. 'You're all right. Quit the kidding. Don't come it, Hughie!'

Savage said nothing.

Percy shook him by the shoulders instead of by the ears, wheedling at him as if he was just trying to waken a heavy sleeper. The body stayed limp, let itself be shaken, gave no answer.

'Oh, my God,' said Percy.

He thought he had killed him. He was willing to admit he had gone too far after all. Whatever his faults, Savage hardly deserved to be murdered for them. Anyway, murder would be an awkward business. It might mean he would never get to his cottage at Land's End.

That was enough to make him move, and move quickly. He groped for his torch and sent the yellow line ahead of him across the cellar to the chute. He was halfway up when he remembered.

'My briefcase!' he cried. 'My cottage.'

He scampered down again, stepped over Savage, grabbed his case, and locked it, standing on one leg, supporting the case on the thigh of the other leg. He was too anxious to get away to think of taking any more money. Up the chute once more he went, his key at the ready. He was just going to put it into the lock and open the door when the door moved in towards him. He was paralysed for a second, then he stepped to one side so that he would be hidden behind the door when it was opened.

A little man in a belted raincoat and cloth cap came through the doorway, stood at the top of the chute and jabbed a flash down into the cellar. It was the inquisitive stranger. Percy recognized the way one foot was turned in a little. It was a time for action, and Percy had never believed that a poet was incapable of action. He swung his briefcase hard against the nape of the stranger's neck, rammed his knee into the small of his back, and pushed him down the chute with every ounce of his strength. The stranger stumbled, tripped, crumpled, and rolled down like a sack of potatoes, crashed at the foot and lay there. Percy dived through the doorway, brought the door to behind him and locked it swiftly.

'He never got a glimpse of me,' he assured himself as he ran down Tulip Place. 'He hasn't a clue what hit him. They can lie there, the pair of them. A couple of rogues. Money, money, money, that's all they could think of. They'd no respect for it, nothing they needed it for like me. They just wanted it. Sheer greed!'

He didn't go home. He loped far away from Tulip Place and Bethel Street, crossed the river and remembering he was a poet he stopped on the bridge for a moment to admire the beauty of the neon ads reflected in the night-dark water. At an open-all-night public convenience near Glasgow Cross he washed his face and combed his hair, removing all signs of his fight with Savage, but he couldn't do much about a dark blue bruise under his eye. Returning to the upper world he struck over towards Charing Cross.

'It's rotten with wee hotels over there,' he told himself. He liked talking to himself, it helped him to work out his plans. 'I'll get a room there for tonight and my breakfast tomorrow and get the ten o'clock to London and I'll find out where to get a train to Land's End. I'm no short of money, that's one good thing.'

He had never slept a night out of his own bed before, and when he stood at the desk in the Kelvin Hotel near Clairmont Gardens he chattered compulsively to hide his nervousness.

'I'm just up from Leeds,' he said. 'Down at my grandmother's funeral. Eighty-seven she was. Going back to Aberdeen first thing the morrow. That's where I live, you see. My train was late getting in. Missed my connexion. Lucky I've got enough money on me to pay for bed and breakfast.'

The night-manager looked at him with weary heavy-lidded eyes. A good look. You never knew when the police would be in the next day asking for a description. There was something odd about this big fellow. Very odd.

'Yes, sir, quite so,' he murmured neutrally, and pushed the register over.

Percy took the offered pen and hesitated. He hadn't thought of this. The manager saw the hesitation, slight as it was, and made a note of Percy's height, colour of his hair and eyes, suit and briefcase, and the big bruise on the right cheek. Percy put the pen to the page.

'Percy Bysshe,' he wrote in the ugly back-hand that used to madden Miss Elginbrod.

The night-manager swivelled the book round with a movement that had all the deftness of routine and glanced at the name.

'And your address in Aberdeen, please,' he said suavely. Bysshe. Who ever heard of such a name? Obviously made up. 'We have to have it in the register, you see. By law. Just in case.'

He stopped, quite enjoying intimidating this lout with the black eye who had given him a lot of gratuitous nonsense about his granny in Leeds and a home in Aberdeen in a voice of the purest Glasgow.

'Oh aye,' said Percy. 'Of course.'

Once more he hesitated. But no dapper little twerp in a dark suit and grey tie, with sleepy eyes and a Kelvinside accent, was going to frighten him. He was no ignorant teddy-boy from a housing-scheme. He was a poet on his way to a poet's cottage. And he had read a bit in his time too. He knew that the motto on the Aberdeen coat of arms was Bon Accord.

'27 Bon Accord Street,' he wrote. Maybe there wasn't actually a Bon Accord Street in Aberdeen, but Bon Accord was Aberdonian enough to serve his turn.

He had done quite well. But then he spoiled it. He read out the address and stressed all the syllables of Bon Accord equally.

'Is that how you say it?' said the manager from somewhere up in the ceiling, far above Percy. 'I thought Aberdonians pronounced it Bunnaccurred.'

He made a dactyl of it. Percy struggled mentally with the

two rhythms. He liked the manager's way of saying it. It flowed.

'Oh aye, they do, of course they do,' he said, grinning like a friendly collie. 'I just said it the other way so you'd recognize it, cause you see these names in print and you never know how to say them till somebody tells you and my writing's not very good. You see I write a lot and it's kind of spoiled my writing. Bunnaccurred of course. Bunnacurred. It's the town motto, you know. It means good accord.'

'Really?' said the night-manager.

The night-porter came up to the desk to take Percy's case and show him to a room.

'Oh no, no thank you,' said Percy, holding the briefcase up and away. 'I'll hang on to this if you don't mind. It's got my grandmother's jewellery in it.'

He couldn't sleep. The bed was too good, it was too clean and comfortable, he felt himself in too strange a world to settle to sleep. Then in the darkness of the strange room he couldn't help thinking of Savage again, and he tossed and turned anxiously. He couldn't believe he had actually killed him, for that was the kind of thing that happened to other people. But even if Savage was lying dead it could never be proved he had murdered him, and since it couldn't be proved then he wasn't guilty. All he had to do was get up sharp in the morning and get away. He had come where life had taken him, and he had still farther to go, he had to get to Land's End and live in exile. When at last he fell over he dreamed of the river all in black running silently through a deserted city, and he was floating down the river in a little boat that wasn't seaworthy, stalked by a stranger who was dead and alive, harmless and dangerous, cunning and stupid. And he was frightened.

The hotel was wrapped in silence like an old woman in a shawl. Only the light in the entrance hall and another in the little office still burned. The night-manager and the night-porter stood on either side of the desk, conversing in whispers.

'There's something funny about him,' said the porter, exbatman to a lieutenant-colonel in the Royal Scots Fusiliers.

'Odd,' said the manager, whilom major in the Army Catering Corps during the second World War.

'You remember that couple last month,' said the porter.

'I'm not likely to forget them,' said the manager.

'Honeymoon couple, all the way from Brighton. Only it was them that did the smash and grab in Romford.'

'The mistake these people make,' said the manager, 'it's a simple one, but they all make it. They think if they come to a quiet little hotel in a backwater like this they'll never be noticed. Whereas of course it's just in a small place like this that we do notice them. That insurance manager last year, the minister and his church organist before that, and that fellow from Ipswich that did in his wife the year before that, and all the rest of them, they all come slinking in here as if they'd come to the end of the line where nobody would ever find them. And an hour after their case is in the papers we're on to them and on to the police.'

'I wonder what he's been up to,' the porter whispered, jerking his thinly thatched dome to the staircase where he had led Percy. 'He doesn't look the violent type, mind you.'

'You never can tell,' said the manager. 'We had a cook once in the Middle East, he looked like a cut-down Mr Pickwick and he put a butcher's chopper through the skull of a mess waiter that was always trying to kid him. He got fed up being kidded, that was all he would say.'

'Well, some of these blokes that are aye at the kidding would get on your nerves,' the porter commented, condoning the murder. 'We had a captain once in my regiment and he was always trying to take the mickey out the RSM. He couldn't ha' done a stupider thing. The upshot was—'

'Yes, I know,' said the manager smoothly. 'You told me. He was beat up in the Schipperstraat in Antwerp and he never knew who did it but he never cracked another joke till he was demobbed.'

The manager withdrew to his little office, and the porter ambled to his corner for a snooze.

And while Percy in the storey above them rose and fell in troubled waves of shallow sleep, like a cork bobbing on the Clyde, Savage still lay still on the stone floor of the cellar. Abandoned by Percy, never missed by his family, he just lay there, a couple of *Sunshine Readers* for his pillow. No comfortable room in a hotel for him, no snow-white sheets and a soft bed, and yet he had just as much money stashed away in an air-raid shelter as Percy had in his briefcase.

Even the stranger hadn't stayed to help him. One look frightened him away. He was only winded when he fell down the chute and he got on his pins cursing and swearing, determined to turn this damned cellar upside down. For all his watching he had never seen anybody go in by the door in Tulip Place, but he had never believed the Phinns' story the door was only a blind. A locksmith friend made half a dozen keys for him, one of which was almost bound to fit the conventional lock on such a door as he had described. He had got the keys that morning, and waited till it was quite dark before trying them. The third one was the lucky one. When it opened the door he felt he was Aladdin entering the cave. The way he was shoved down the chute the moment he put a foot across the threshold convinced him someone was trying to keep him out of the cellar. Which in turn proved that the cellar was the right place, as he had suspected all along.

He too had come furnished with a torch, a bigger and better one than Percy's or Savage's, and he used it to probe the extent of the cellar when he staggered to his feet. He was ready and willing to take all night to searching it. But when he saw a schoolboy in a black leather jacket and jeans lying huddled against a pile of rubbish his heart came up to his gullet, turned over, and fell to the pit of his stomach.

Whether the boy was dead or dying was no concern of his. It was enough there was a body lying there. He had his own pride in his intelligence, and his guess was that two other folk had found the money before him and one of them had done in the other.

'Just my bloody luck!' he moaned. 'Just that bit too late.

The bastard that wired me must ha' been on his way out with the lot. So help ma Bob!'

He flashed a beam of daylight brightness on Savage, up and down him and round him, and bent over him a little. He thought he heard breathing but he couldn't wait to make sure. He didn't want to get involved. To hang around murder or manslaughter or whatever it was would put him out of the way of the money for ever. He left Savage lying and scrambled up the chute, practically on all fours, back to his kennel in a motel near Bridgeton Cross.

The sun rose again in a clear sky, promising another hot day, and Percy rose with it, not refreshed but not fatigued. He washed and shaved slowly, wallowing in the luxury of his first morning in a hotel. He was all set for his flight to London and from there to Land's End. His scalp tingled, as often before, with a thrilling sensation that fate had marked him out for something special. He was no commonplace non-entity from a back-street. He had a destiny, and he had the talisman of his briefcase. He wasn't sure how many thousands were in it, for the fight with Savage had confused his memory, but he was sure he had enough to arm him for a long time against an unfriendly world. He thought he could live for years on what he was carrying, and he couldn't think past that.

He had his breakfast in a corner of a heavily quiet dining-room, a gaunt clergyman and his chubby wife in another corner, two debonair commercial travellers in a third, and an elderly couple who looked like Punch and Judy living in retirement slobbered softly in the fourth corner. The centre was a desert of white tablecloths and glittering cutlery. Grapefruit or porridge, toast, and bacon and eggs. Percy chose the grapefruit because he had never liked porridge and then he had difficulty scooping out a spoonful. He let it go half-eaten, but made up for it on the toast and bacon and eggs.

The night-manager was still on duty and when Percy passed the desk on his way out to Charing Cross and a bus to the Central Station he sent a weary glance from under his heavy-lidded eyes, and a little smile flickered under his pencil-line moustache.

'Good morning, sir,' he said gently. 'Pleasant journey to Aberdeen.'

Percy splayed manfully on.

'Morning,' he muttered audibly, and inaudibly he said, 'Sarcastic little nyaff. You'd think he didn't believe I was going to Aberdeen.'

It was just turned nine o'clock on a bright summer morning in the middle of June.

CHAPTER FOURTEEN

So bright was the morning that elderly men went to work without a hat and without a waistcoat, young girls bloomed at the bus-stops in sleeveless frocks and bare legs, glad to leave off their stockings because it meant they didn't need to wear a girdle, schoolboys who had sat their term examinations played truant along the banks of the Canal as far north as Bishopbriggs and Cawder, and the city reeled in a heat haze filled with the choking smell of dust and tar. The cruel sun put a limelight on the decaying front of slum properties where housewives eighty feet above the gutters sweated in a love-longing for the country and listened to the pigeons moaning, all in the blue unclouded weather.

Before nine o'clock Mr Daunders had two phone calls. The first was from Miss Nairn's mother to say Miss Nairn wouldn't be in because she had flu.

'Flu in the month of June!' Mr Daunders muttered callously when he put the phone back in its cradle. 'Flu in weather like this! What will they think up next?'

He sat chafing at his little desk and tried to work out a way of dispersing Miss Nairn's class amongst the other teachers without coming into collision with the noncooperative element. He had nearly finished allotting the last half-dozen of Miss Nairn's forty-eight pupils when he had his second phone call. Mr Whiffen said he wouldn't be in till some time after ten or eleven because his widowed mother had taken a bad turn during the night and he had to wait in for the doctor to call. There was no one else.

Mr Daunders sneered at the phone sceptically when he cradled it again, and sat at his desk to work out what to do about Mr Whiffen's forty-five pupils.

'He probably means he won't be in all morning, if I know him,' he snorted. 'Now what's the best thing to do? I don't want to disperse another class. I've nowhere to put them even if I did. What I could do is shift an infant-teacher into Whiffen's class for the morning, and put six girls from the top class into the infants. It would serve. They could keep them quiet or play games with them. Oh, if I could just find peace and quiet to sit in the sun and read my Horace! Aye, the far Coolins are calling me away!'

He went out to the playground at nine o'clock to see the school in and strolled back in the sunshine to his room. Maybe he could get peace for an hour or two now. But when he entered the corridor where his room was he saw a man and a woman waiting at his door. He hadn't his glasses on and he peered. He sensed trouble. He relaxed a little when he recognized Frank Garson and his father. They wouldn't be bringing trouble. They were nice people.

'Beautiful morning,' he said pleasantly, raising his grey felt hat to the lady. 'Can I help you, Mr Garson?'

'This is my wife,' said Mr Garson. 'She thought we ought to come and see you. I kept the boy back, to come with us, I hope you don't mind, but you see it's him that's the reason for us wanting to see you. It's him that knows what my wife thinks you ought to be told. He's got a story about the cellar.'

'The cellar?' said Mr Daunders. 'Come in. Come in, Mrs Garson. You mean the school cellar?'

'I'm afraid so,' said Mr Garson unhappily, and threw an appeal at his wife to take over. She knew he hated talking.

That was her line, and this was her idea. His wife raised her head high with pride, taking her cue, knowing this was her hour, and started talking calmly, fluently, clearly, with a don't-you-dare-interrupt-me firmness.

Mr Daunders hunched at his desk and played with his paper-knife as she talked. Apart from the fact that he prided himself on always letting other people have their say and believed he had a cool, analytical brain that could extract the essence from any amount of blethering, he was in no state to interrupt. As soon as she mentioned money hidden in the cellar his head was a battlefield of different pains struggling for supremacy; a dogged steady ache holding its ground like fire-baptised infantry grimly obstructed the sudden sallies that thrust deep into his skull like a combined air and tank force blitzing the infantry.

'I knew it, I knew it, I knew it,' he muttered, not interrupting her, merely making a light marginal note to her narrative as she described the share-out. He ploughed his grey hair with clean-nailed fingers and turned to the boy when the mother finished.

'Just how much would you say was there?' he asked sadly.

Frank Garson knew he had to go through with it now it was started, but he wasn't enjoying being an informer. He looked at his headmaster dully and said nothing.

'A hundred?' Mr Daunders bid.

The boy shook a heavy head.

'A thousand?' Mr Daunders raised his bid.

The boy looked at him as if he was daft.

'Ten, twenty or thirty, I don't know,' he gave a grudging answer.

'Thousand?' Mr Daunders' eyebrows went up. 'You mean thousands, you don't mean just ten or twenty pounds?'

'Thousands,' the boy insisted softly.

Mr Daunders sagged over his paper-knife.

'Now, think, my boy, think!' he admonished him magisterially. 'Maybe there's not much between ten and twenty pounds, but there's a big difference between ten thousand

and twenty thousand. As for thirty thousand, now just think! Thirty thousand is twenty thousand more than ten thousand.'

The boy didn't dispute it.

'You surely know better than that how much you saw,' Mr Daunders said plaintively.

'It was an awful lot,' the boy said helpfully.

'We'd better go down and see this cellar,' said Mr Daunders bravely rising.

He sent for the janitor to bring the key, and they all went down through the basement, Mr and Mrs Garson, Frank and the headmaster, and Mr Green the janitor leading them with the key in his hand like a mace-bearer leading a royal procession. Once the door was opened Mr Green switched on the ceiling lights and ushered them all in. He was glad he had the foresight to put a team of cleaners on to tidying the place. His conscience was clear. He didn't mind who inspected the cellar.

'It's a bit dusty,' he said pleasantly, 'but I try to keep it in some kind of order. It was just a dump before I came here. What was it you were wanting to see, Mr Daunders?'

The headmaster wasn't disposed to tell the janitor more in the meantime than he had to.

'It's only something this boy thinks he saw down here,' he said remotely. 'Just wait by the door, Mr Green, please, if you don't mind.'

But before Frank Garson had time to cross the cellar and point out the tea-chests they all saw Savage lying on the floor. Mr Daunders cried, 'Oh, my God!' Mrs Garson screamed, Mr Garson frowned, the janitor came forward from the door, eager for sensation, and Frank Garson fainted.

The mother attended to her boy and the janitor attended to Savage. Like all janitors he was a bit of a plumber, electrician, carpenter, glazier, accountant, wages-clerk, and first-aid expert.

'He's all right,' he said on his knees. 'He's breathing. He's knocked out or fainted or something.'

Mr Daunders hopped bird-like round the kneeling janitor and the prostrate boy.

'Phone for an ambulance,' he cried anxiously, 'phone for the police, get his mother, take him up to my room, get a doctor, quick!'

'Well, give us a hand then,' said Mr Green, slightly aggrieved at the number of orders.

Mr Garson thawed far enough to help him to carry the boy upstairs. Frank Garson came to and followed them with his mother's right arm round his shoulders, and Mr Daunders guarded the rear from further alarms.

'Just remembered,' panted the janitor as he laboured up the steep staircase from the cellar to the basement while Mr Garson grunted with Savage's feet against his midriff. 'This is the school doctor's morning, the monthly medical, you know. Maybe he's in by this time.'

All Mr Daunders' orders were obeyed, not all at once, but in due order. They laid Savage reverently on the floor in Mr Daunders' room, they fetched the school visiting doctor from the medical room, they phoned for an ambulance, and they sent the school milk attendant to fetch in Mrs Savage. The call to the police Mr Daunders put off for a while till he had time to take his bearings.

The doctor said it was only a case of concussion. Mrs Savage said the boy hadn't been home all night but she hadn't worried, because it wasn't the first time he had run away and he always came back, and the ambulance took him to the Royal Infirmary.

'Now,' sighed Mr Daunders, hunched at his desk again. 'Where are we?'

'Look, Mr Daunders,' said the janitor shrewdly. 'That boy was in a fight. Cause I saw his belt lying beside him when we picked him up. You know that belt you told him not to wear, that Army belt with all the brass studs in it, it was lying near him. I bet you he took it off to swipe somebody and got the worst of it. But I don't know how he got into the cellar, there's only me got a key to it.'

He was in on this and he wasn't going to be kept out. No

standing by at the door for him, he was on the inside now. After all, it was his cellar. You couldn't have boys lying unconscious in his cellar, and then try and tell him to wait outside please. No, thank you.

'There's something queer going on,' he said. 'You mark my words.'

'Let's go back down,' said Mr Daunders patiently. It couldn't be kept from the janitor. There was no point trying. 'Are you all right now, Frank?'

The boy nodded, standing in front of his mother with her hands on his shoulder, nestling into her like a frightened sparrow.

'Yes, he's all right now,' said his mother. 'That would have given anybody a shock, so it would. He might have been dead for all we knew. But we want to get this story cleared up one way or the other.'

They all went back to the cellar, with Frank as the fingerman. One chest was empty, the next had three hundred and fifty pounds, and the third had two hundred and seventy. The janitor was astounded, Frank was humiliated, and his parents and Mr Daunders looked at him with respect. To them, his story was proved. He had merely mistaken hundreds for thousands, a thing any schoolboy might do at the sight of a lot of money.

'Good God, what an amount of money!' cried Mr Green, and rubbed his chin with itching fingers.

'Somebody's been at it,' Frank Garson whispered. 'Somebody's shifted it.'

'Was there more?' Mr Daunders asked softly.

'A wheen mair, I mean a lot more,' the boy told him, almost angrily. 'And there was money in the chest that's empty. I know. I tried to count it once. And I saw it at the last Friday Night Service.'

'The last what?' Mr Daunders frowned.

'This boy Phinn was starting a new religion,' Mrs Garson explained. 'That's a part of the story I didn't make clear when I was talking to you.'

'Yes, of course, this fellow Percy Phinn was the ringleader, wasn't he?' Mr Daunders remembered. His head was giving him hell. 'I'd better send across the street for his mother. I know her. And I'll have to phone the police. I'm sorry, Mrs Garson, but I'll have to.'

'I don't mind,' she answered proudly. 'My boy's hands are clean.'

'Leave those chests just as they are, Mr Green,' the head-master addressed the janitor formally. 'Lock the door after us and give me the key. I want things left just as they are for the police.'

He sent the Garsons home. The parents said they were afraid of reprisals if their boy stayed on at the school. He told them to get a medical certificate for him.

'Nerves, general debility, anything you like,' he said. 'It doesn't matter. There are only two weeks left till the end of term. And he's sat all his examinations. It doesn't matter. He would be safer away till all this is sorted out. You're quite right.'

'We're moving anyway,' Mr Garson chipped in so unex-pectedly that Mr Daunders turned to him as to a dumb stranger who had suddenly acquired the gift of speech. 'I'm getting a job outside the city, and I'm going to put the boy to another school after the holidays.'

'An excellent idea,' said Mr Daunders. He was too con-cerned about the police calling at his school to care very much where Frank Garson went next session.

'There must have been nearly a thousand quid there,' said Mr Green chattily when the Garsons were gone and Mr Daunders stood at the phone dialling the police.

'Would you mind running across the street and asking Mrs Phinn to come over and see me for a moment?' he said, freezing him.

Mrs Phinn came over in her slippers and an old black dress that was torn under one arm-pit. She knew nothing of any money. She was only a poor despised widow, forced by poverty to work as a cleaner in the school where her man had once been the janitor, and a far better janitor than Mr Green would ever be, a janitor headmasters could turn to for advice. All she knew was Percy hadn't been home all night, and he was a good son and he had never stayed away all night before. Where was Mr Daunders hiding him? What was he trying to do to her?

'You know more about him than I do,' she said aggressively. 'Bringing me over here to ask me a lot of questions. And you know the answers, I can tell it the way you ask me. What are you trying to make me say?'

She didn't do Mr Daunders' headache any good, and he was glad to get rid of her without telling her very much.

'We thought you might be able to help us, that's all. It's nothing much, not really. No more than I've tried to tell you, if you'd only listen. There's been some money hidden in the cellar and some boys said Percy knew something about it. We're not accusing anybody, we just wanted to have a word with your son.'

Mrs Phinn was as keen to get away as Mr Daunders was to let her go. She didn't want to listen to any talk of money in the cellar. The moment he mentioned it she remembered the stranger in the raincoat. She was sure it meant real trouble now, and all she wanted to do was bury her head in the sand of her own corner till it was all over.

'I always knew that big stupid lump would get into trouble one day,' she muttered, banging the door behind when she got home. 'Him and his books, as thick as his head. Ideas above his station, that's his trouble. And where the hell has he got to? Well, he won't break my heart, I'll make sure of that. And me sticking up for him, telling folk he's a good son. He's been a dead loss since the day I weaned him!'

Mr Daunders relaxed for a moment or two in the blessed silence of his room when Mrs Phinn had gone.

'I suppose I'll have to phone the Office too,' he thought, sighing in misery. He had always made it his policy never to bother the Director of Education. 'See what they think. They may want a formal report. I don't know what the procedure is in a case like this. But that cellar is Corporation property, so I suppose the Office has a legal interest in the money. Found on their property. I wonder whose it is? But I can't see that I'm responsible in any way. Oh dear, what a mess! By God, I'll enjoy this summer holiday. A fine quiet month in Skye, far away from it all!'

While he was waiting for the police to arrive he sent for Noddy, Specky, Skinny, Wedderburn, Cuddie and Cutchy – all the boys mentioned in Mrs Garson's account of what her son had told her, and all the boys he had found with too much money at one time or another. He saw them one by one, keeping them incommunicado till his interviews were complete. He questioned them cleverly, he wheedled and coaxed, he shouted and whispered, he threatened and promised, adjusting his technique to the temperament of the boy. He learned nothing. Maybe they weren't very bright at the general analysis of a complex sentence or the decimalization of money, but they knew when the wind was in the east. They had their own grapevine. They didn't know Savage had been found knocked out in the cellar, but they all knew Savage was absent. They had all seen Garson waiting with his father and mother at the headmaster's door. They didn't know why. But they all knew Garson hadn't gone to his class after that. They saw their cue and they took it. There is nobody shrewder than a backward schoolboy. It may be an awkward fact, but it is still a fact, that when a boy has a battle of wits with his headmaster, even if that headmaster is an Honours graduate in Latin and Greek with a pass in the classes of Logic and Metaphysics and Mental Philosophy, the boy wins every time. He isn't tempted to parry and equivocate, he doesn't feel any desire to show off and come back with a clever answer. He is a brick wall, and you can't see through a brick wall by logic alone. You need a window.

Mr Daunders dismissed the last of them and prepared a memorandum for the police. Two plain-clothes men called just before the morning interval and made Mr Daunders' little office look tiny indeed. He sat at his desk rather than stand up beside them, five feet seven against six feet one and six feet two. They made notes in a little notebook as he went through his narrative.

'Looks like your boy Savage had a fight with this fellow Percy in the cellar last night,' said one of them, thrusting his notebook into the inside pocket of his jacket. 'They had a fight over the money. Let's have a look at it, please.'

Mr Daunders took them down to the cellar, and when they saw it they glanced at each other and nodded.

'Yes, we know where this came from,' said the one who hadn't spoken before.

'What we want to know is how it got here, of course,' said the other.

They climbed the steep staircase to the basement again and went back to the headmaster's room. Before lunch-time they had questioned all the boys Mr Daunders had tried to question. And Noddy, Specky, Skinny, Wedderburn, Cuddy and Cutchy who had stonewalled Mr Daunders' bowling, didn't raise a bat when the two plain-clothes men got to work on them. There's nobody like a plain-clothes man for getting a Glasgow schoolboy to come clean. Stringing a teacher along is all part of the natural order of things, but he doesn't like taking a chance with a detective. The law-man always wins. The telly had taught him that, even if it had taught him nothing more.

'Looks like this fellow Percy is our man,' said the taller detective when the three of them were alone again. 'I don't think he knows where it came from. It looks like he just found it. But it seems pretty certain he organized these lads to spend it and then blew with the rest of it. He's probably got thousands. We'll push off to the infirmary and see if this boy Savage is fit to talk to. I think he guessed what Percy was up to and they had a fight about it.'

'Oh, this Phinn fellow won't get very far,' said the other plain-clothes man. 'We've got a good description. We'll pick him up by tea-time. You can't escape the police today. Telephones, radio, television. Wherever he goes he'll be recognized. He hasn't a chance.'

'No,' said Mr Daunders. 'There's no escape, is there? Not for any of us.'

The two plain-clothes men took leave of Mr Daunders graciously. They were polite and unexcitable. They knew they were on the winning side.

'Of course, Callum,' said the one to the other on the way out, 'we don't know that Phinn will be able to tell us how it got there.'

'No, that's true, Ewan,' answered his mate. 'But he must know something surely. Anyway, before we go to the infirmary let's get his description out. London, Dublin, Belfast, Liverpool, the Channel Ports, the works.'

CHAPTER FIFTEEN

Percy felt fine travelling first-class to London. He would have treated himself to travelling by air but he didn't know if you had to book in advance, and he had no time to find out. The train was so quiet he had a compartment to himself, and he sat back enjoying his solitary comfort. This was the life. This was the beginning of his long-desired peace and quiet. Between Glasgow and Kilmarnock he was thrilled with the speed of the train and gazed through the window with childish interest at the circular sweep of the countryside as it rushed past him. He felt the blue unclouded sky above the fields was blessing his journey and he marvelled at the way the train was devouring distance. He had never been so far from home before and his journey was hardly started. He fetched out a little diary with a map of the British Isles on the front fly-leaf and studied his route.

'Morning coffee,' intoned a man in a white jacket, sliding the door half-open and then passed on lurching smoothly to the roll of the train.

'Sure thing,' said Percy brightly.

He took his briefcase with him. Maybe he wasn't a poet, maybe he was a promising young executive on his way to a conference in London. He put a distant look in his eyes as he sat alone at a table for two, his precious briefcase snugly between his side and the window. The waiter would recognize he had problems on his mind, business problems, and his case contained the documents he had to study.

'White or black?' said the waiter, two jugs at the ready.

Percy found it a difficult question. He had never been served that way before. All his mother ever made was tea and all Sophy ever gave him was espresso coffee. He wondered which was the more sophisticated choice.

'Black if you don't mind,' he said at last with ungainly assumption of nonchalance.

He fumbled badly taking a couple of biscuits from the tray offered him and grew cross with himself. Anybody carrying the amount of money he was carrying had no call to get nervous. Then he made a problem out of the tip. The bill was one and six, and he had a florin and a half-crown handy. Sixpence seemed too mean a tip, too Scots for a poet on his way to Cornwall, so he put both coins down and waved away the change like a pasha dismissing an unsatisfactory dancing-girl.

He spent the time between morning coffee and lunch brooding about it. Maybe he had tipped him too much. There was something in the arch of the waiter's shaggy eyebrows. He had read in a magazine that the proper tip was ten per cent of the bill. Ten per cent of one and six was quite a sum for him to work out in his head. The only answer he could get sounded absurd and the calculation reminded him of Miss Elginbrod so he gave it up. Anyway, a poet was above arithmetic. There was that great French writer he had read of who used to tip the waiter at the Ritz extravagantly. If he had over-tipped he was in good company.

Lunch came along accompanied with more problems. He felt clumsy with the soup spoon, awkward with the knife and fork, ill-at-ease with the dessert spoon. He would willingly have settled for his mother's stand-by of mince and tatties followed by a cup of tea with no saucer. But there was no tea to follow. It was coffee again.

It was afternoon tea finally shattered him. He was bewildered by the accent of a waiter he had seen from a distance at lunch.

'Teakike aw taoust?' he asked, bowing over him with a large tray balanced in one hand and a serving-fork in the other.

Percy didn't recognize the language. The cockney diphthong echoed and echoed in his head till in sheer fatigue it resolved itself into a good round long 'o'.

'Toast,' said Percy severely, resenting the accent.

He was left with his toast, a little china teapot and a small jar of apple jelly. The train barged on, exulting in its freedom, and it gave a heave and a sway like a wild mustang every time Percy lifted the teapot and tried to pour himself a cup of tea. He got more tea in the saucer than in the cup, and when he raised the cup and tried to find the rim with his lips drops of spilt tea fell on his lap. He decided to do without a cup of tea and eased some jelly from the jar with his knife. He nearly had it safe on his toast when the train did another bucking-bronco act, and the quivering jelly slid off his knife, missed his toast and his plate and landed plop on the white cloth. He scooped it off hastily and felt the cockney waiter's eyes squinting at him. To assert himself and demonstrate his natural dexterity he lifted the teapot again. It was worse than the first time. He didn't only miss the cup, he missed the saucer too. The waiter came over with unostentatious grace, murmured, 'Excuse me, sir,' removed the swimming saucer and dripping cup, and came back with another cup and saucer. Silently he poured Percy a cup of tea from the little pot without spilling a drop.

Percy was humiliated. He felt all his self-esteem and all the confidence built by the money in the briefcase evaporate like moisture under a blazing sun. And the sudden evaporation chilled him to the marrow. He began to feel afraid.

When he stepped off the train and walked through Euston Station the weakening of his confidence cracked to a complete failure of nerve. What had seemed a vague and distant future, fit material for daydreams, was now a precise and immediate problem. It was all very well saying he was going to Land's End, but just exactly where and how would he live when he got there? What would he do? He had fallen from the clouds and had to pick his way on the ground. He didn't like it. There was no breakfast, dinner and tea, no laundry and rent, no strangers to meet and no bills to pay in his daydreams. But they were all worrying him now, little daily chores he would have to face, and he didn't feel fit to cope. It wasn't enough just having the money. He had to get organized.

He took a taxi, his first taxi, to Victoria. He had picked up the idea somewhere that Victoria was the right station for the west country.

'Oh, blimey!' said the taxi-driver when Percy paid the fare with one of the fivers he had shoved into his pocket in the cellar. 'What's this? A soap coupon?'

'That's a perfectly good five-pound note,' Percy told him severely, rebellious at his flippancy.

'Yus, but taint an English fiver,' the taxi-driver retorted. 'It's the foreign exchange you want, mate. I don't reckon on changing fivers every trip, not Scotch ones, anyway. Is that all you've got?'

'Yes, it's all I've got,' Percy admitted, and his head was hot and his face was red. To prove he was telling the truth he fished out the handfuls of fivers he had stuffed in his pocket.

'Whatja bin doing? Robbin a bank?' asked the taxi-driver pleasantly. 'Youghta changed all that foreign money before you came down here, son.'

He changed the note with a grudge, and when he had turned round in a curve hardly bigger than the arc of a Scots threepenny-bit and dashed back into Victoria Street he left a very worried Percy outside the Station.

'I never thought on that,' he meditated, alone and bewildered. 'I should've got travellers' cheques, so I should. But then I'd have to have banked it, wouldn't I? And I couldn't just walk into a bank and bank thousands in fivers. That would have put the ba' up on the slates, that would! I should have studied banking instead of reading so much philosophy. I might have found a way round it then.'

He turned his back on the station and trudged along Victoria Street, making trivial purchases here and there and changing a fiver each time. Between the difficulty caused by his accent and the strangeness of the currency he tendered, he had a rough time. He was made to feel his notes were being changed this time as a favour, but he wasn't to do it again.

He became so confused he forgot he had taken a taxi to get him to Victoria, and kept slouching on away from the Station. When he came to Parliament Square and Westminster Bridge the tea-time rush was at its thickest. He stood at the pavement edge, afraid to cross the road. He was a Gulliver among the Brobdingnagians. All these smart, elegant young men, these slim swift girls, seemed a superior race. Glasgow was a village in comparison, and he wished he was back there. By the time he had walked round Parliament Square and managed to get across to Westminster Bridge to look at the Thames he was lost. He wasn't sure if Victoria Station was behind or in front of him, to his right or his left. Half an hour in London had shattered him. He fought back bravely for a moment by going up to one of the smart elegant young men in black jacket, striped trousers and bowler, with a rolled umbrella in hand, and asked him how to get to Victoria Station. It was only another defeat. The elegant young man couldn't understand a word of Percy's broad Glasgow and Percy couldn't understand a word of the elegant young man's Lambeth (In fact all he said was, 'I'm sorry, I don't speak French.')

More by good luck than guidance he got back on his tracks again and his weary splay feet took him slowly back along Victoria Street. He was tired, hot and sticky, but he didn't dare take a bus because he didn't know which one to take, and he was sure he wouldn't know where to get off anyway. One thing was certain, he wasn't going to ask any of these foreigners to direct him a second time. Nobody could make out what they were saying. You asked them a simple question and you got a lot of gibberish back. Walking was safer.

The Station frightened him when he saw it again. It was a jungle of people. He could never fight his way through there. He didn't even try. He kept on prowling, thinking he would rest in an hotel for the night and enquire in the morning how to get to Land's End. A small place in Wilton Road took his fancy and he sidled through the glass door into a hushed house with thick carpets. A dapper little man behind a highly polished counter greeted him in a benevolent whisper, and Percy nervously explained he had left Aberdeen in a hurry on an urgent business matter and hadn't had time to change his Scottish fivers to English ones. He showed a handful to prove he could pay for a room. 'Would you accept these...' He faded away like a radio with a defective valve.

'Oh, yes, of course. That's quite all right,' the dapper little man said courteously. With an ear accustomed to divers accents he got a working idea of what Percy was trying to say. The only thing that puzzled him was why a youth with an unmistakable Glasgow voice should say he had come from Aberdeen.

He pushed the register across, and Percy signed his own name, too worn out to think what he was doing.

He lay on top of his bed for an hour, his shoes and socks off, wiggling his toes to cool his fiery feet. London's pavements were hotter than Glasgow's. He slid into a little doze and disorderly pictures of Savage passed over his exhausted brain. Then slowly, for all his morning coffee, his three-course lunch and his afternoon tea, an appetite uncoiled in him and he had a craving for a fish supper. Surely in a big city like London he could buy a poke of fish and chips somewhere. He certainly didn't want dinner in the hotel. What he had seen of the dining room when he was being shown upstairs to his room had been enough for him. He didn't want a snow-white cloth and a spread of gleaming cutlery. He just wanted a poke of fish and chips, and maybe a cup of tea.

He heaved himself up with a sigh and sat on the edge of his bed, shoving his fingers through his straw-coloured hair and yawning. When the long groaning yawn was spent he bent down to pick up his sweat-damp socks from the floor.

'I should buy another pair of socks, that's what I should do,' he thought, groping wearily.

There was a knock at his door. He froze, still bent down, one hand clutching one sock. He straightened slowly, holding his breath.

'Aye?' he called out hoarsely, puzzled.

Two men came in. Two tall, broad-shouldered men, clean shaven and alert, bareheaded, one just a little grey, the other red-haired. For all his sheltered life Percy knew two plain-clothes policemen when he saw them.

'Ye didn't take long, did ye?' he said, his bare feet on the carpet with the toes clenched.

He looked at them plaintively and began to cry. He was tired and fed up.

'Percy Phinn?' said the grey-haired man.

'Is he dead?' Percy asked, still clutching his sock. The sole was hard where the sweat had dried. His answering one question by asking another was involuntary. He wasn't deliberately stalling. He was worried about Savage.

They didn't know what he was talking about. All they had was Percy's description and the information that he would probably be carrying a lot of money that wasn't his own. It was all the hotel-manager had too when he phoned them. Percy didn't know he was famous at last, just as he had longed to be, named and described on radio and television. He hadn't thought of his flight being public knowledge by tea-time. What he thought was that only murder could have brought the police on to him so quickly.

'Is who dead?' the grey-haired man asked gently.

'Savage,' said Percy with a quivering lower lip. 'You know about Savage. Did I kill him? I never meant to. It was an accident.'

'We just want to ask you a few questions,' the policeman said soothingly. He preferred to let the question of Savage lapse till he learned more. 'May I see your luggage, please?'

Percy began to cry again, with such childish abandonment that they had to take time off to comfort him. They weren't cruel men. They didn't enjoy seeing a big fellow like Percy in such a state.

'Come on, come on now! Pull yourself together!' said the red-haired man. 'If you'd killed anybody we would know about it. We just want to have a chat with you. Come on now, you're all right now!'

Percy watched them take his briefcase and open it. His sobs died away. He put on his socks and shoes and stood up, willing to go. He knew he had lost the briefcase for good. It was like having a bad tooth pulled. Courage screwed to the sticking point, panic in the pit of his stomach, and then the grinding loss and the relief, the consolation of knowing he would be better off without it, the suffering over.

He felt very important being taken away in a police-car, and when he sat in the police-station answering questions he was anxious to be friendly. He wanted to impress these two kind gentlemen who had treated him so courteously. They gave him a cup of tea. They even got a fish supper for him. He was grateful. He owed it to them to make it clear he was no dumb delinquent from a Glasgow slum. No, he was an intelligent youth with a good command of English. All the doubts that had obscurely budded within him during his journey south in the Royal Scot, all the dim misgivings that had thrown a deathly shadow over his self-esteem, the frightening sensation of being a Lilliputian in Brobdingnag when he left Euston Station, all these made him eager to surrender. But to surrender with dignity. The bubbling stream of his fluency surprised himself, and he was proud to be so clear and honest.

The two policemen listened so attentively he was sure he had captured their interest by his gift for expression. Partly they had to concentrate to understand what he was saying in his outlandish voice, partly they knew there was a time to stop asking questions and just let him ramble. He rambled. Behind him another policeman sat at a small table taking shorthand notes, but Percy was so taken up with his defence that he didn't even notice him.

'Mind you, I see the fallacy,' he said. He liked the word. It was an honest admission of error. 'I like to give in to a fair thing. Money won't make you a poet or a philosopher. You've got to have genius or well anyway talent and when you have it you've still got to work. To use it, I mean, to make anything of it, you've got to work. You just can't run away with money. What did I want the money for anyway? Well, I'll tell you. I wanted to get peace and quiet. Peace and quiet to be a poet or something. Aye, but then when you've got the peace and quiet you've got to make use of it, you've got to do something, you've got to work. Money'll give you leisure but the leisure's no use if you haven't got the genius. And when you haven't got it, money's no substitute. I had been reading a lot of Shelley, cause he's got the same name as me, the same colour of hair, and he had the money to do what he wanted, so I thought if I had the money I could do what Shelley done. But you see that's the fallacy I was telling you about. The money itself won't do it, you've got to be born to it. It's all a matter of birth. You've got to be born to the use of money just like you've got to be born with genius. You take the folk that win the pools. I read an article once and it showed that ninety-nine-point-nine of the folk that win the big money in the pools never come to anything. Mind you, I didn't want the money for materialistic purposes. No, what I'm telling you is I've got spiritualistic values. I wanted the money to get peace and quiet, to write my poetry, you understand. And then coming down in the train today it dawned on me I hadn't a pome in my head. I've wrote nothing since I found the money. I'm not a poet, I'm not a philosopher. You've got to be born to these things. It's all a matter of heredity. There's no use kidding and swanking. My father was only a plumber and then he was a janitor and my mother worked in Templeton's carpet factory before she was married. You see, I'd need a different hereditary, but then I wouldn't be me, would I? Mind you, I'm clever enough, I'm not stupid, but money won't make you a poet, will it? It won't even get you peace and quiet when you're not born to the use of it.'

'So you found this money?' said the grey-haired man.

'No, I never found it,' said Percy quickly. 'One of the Brotherhood found it, and it was reported to me because I tried to learn them and I had to take charge of the money for their own good.'

'Did your father ever mention it to you?' asked the red-haired man.

'Oh no,' said Percy, almost laughing at the idea. 'My father never mentioned anything to me. He was a sort of quiet man. He never spoke to me much.'

'Well, where do you think it came from?' asked the red-haired man.

'Now, that's a good point,' said Percy eagerly. 'Now, you might think this a bit far-fetched but I feel very serious about it. I believe it came from God like the manna to the Jews in the desert. We were all in the desert. We never had a thing. And I believed God chose me, 'cause God does choose people, doesn't He? I mean, you can't deny it, can you? You take Moses.'

The two policemen looked at him steadily, showing no inclination to take anybody.

'Do you know El is the Hebrew word for God?' Percy asked them in the tone of a person who is sure the answer is No. 'And El is the sign of the pound note. You know that much, don't you? Well, I believed the God of Moses had revealed Himself to me under the form of El. I had a regular service every Friday night, I taught piety to the Brotherhood, but they fell away, just like the Jews did with Moses. I was the only one that was true to God. I believe in

God, you know. I'm not an atheist. I'm not one of your juvenile delinquents. I've studied things. Maybe my God's not your God but He's still God, and I'll grant you your God's God too. But my fallacy was . . .'

He was off again in a circle, and the policemen let him talk till he dried up. In the morning they took him back to Glasgow.

CHAPTER SIXTEEN

Savage came to just about the time Percy was having lunch on the Royal Scot. He was foxed for a while to find himself in a clean bed all to himself, wearing a night-shirt he had never worn before, and he sniffed curiously at the strange smell of the place. It was an odd stink, like strong soap. Then it all came back and he knew where he was. When the nurse who saw he was conscious at last brought in a policeman to see him he was too crafty to talk. He pretended he had lost his memory.

'Don't remember,' he mumbled in reply to every question.

He stayed in hospital all that day, and slept there that night, still pretending to be very groggy. There wasn't a thing wrong with him, but he knew the policeman would come back and he wanted time to think what to do.

'Hey, hey!' he called his nurse over with rude insistence at breakfast time. 'I've got to get up, I've got to get outa here. My memory's come back. I've gotta go and tell the polis what I know. They're waiting for me to help them.'

He was so eager, and he looked so innocent and well, they discharged him. But he didn't go near the police, he didn't go home, and he didn't go to school. He wandered round the fruit-market, stole a turnip just for practice, strolled over to the docks and bought a hot pie and a cup of tea in a poky little café in Anderston. He felt thrilled with the delight of freedom, happy with a plan that was funny enough to make a cat laugh. He sang to himself with the joy of it, hopped and skipped, chuckled and rubbed his palms together. Life was good and the sky shared his pleasure, flung wide over him without a cloud in it.

He turned up in Bethel Street at tea-time and the bush telegraph went to work so quickly that he had most of the Brotherhood at his appointed meeting-place within quarter of an hour. They came in ones and two across the waste ground between the Steamie and the back-courts of Bethel Street, silent, worried, waiting the words of wisdom from the great Savage, Senior Claviger of the Bethel Brotherhood.

Specky came forward with his right hand high.

'Hail!' he said with an ingratiating smirk.

'Hail,' Savage murmured, his hand barely lifted. 'Whadya know?'

'Garson shopped us,' said Specky.

'He did, did he?' said Savage. He sneered briefly. 'Don't worry. I'll get that little lilyfaced come-to-Jesus bastard yet. I'll tie his guts round his neck, so I will. Don't worry. I'll sort him all right.'

Skinny was only a step behind Specky.

'Whadya know?' Savage greeted him too impartially, lounging against the wall of the air-raid shelter.

'It's in the papers,' Skinny said mournfully. 'And it was on the Scottish news on the telly there the now. They've got Percy. He's been arrested. They got him in London last night. Imagine our Percy in London!'

'Scotland's secret weapon.' Savage murmured lazily.

'He stole all our money and done a bunk,' said Skinny.

Savage grinned wisely.

'The game's up,' said Specky. 'The cellar's finished. There's been cops there all day. You'd think the school was a police-station, the bobbies that's there.'

'You don't want to worry about the cellar,' said Savage.

'Well, we canny get in there now,' Specky complained.

'So what?' Savage asked, very uppish with him. 'There's nothing there now.'

'No, it looks like Percy cleaned it out,' said Skinny.

'I cleaned it out,' Savage boasted quickly. 'I've got ten times more stashed away than Percy took. I'm the boss now, Percy's a dead loss.'

'But the game's up,' Specky repeated. 'We couldny use it now. The cops is on to it. They'll be wanting to see you. They've seen us, all of us, even that nit Noddy.'

'What did yous tell them?' Savage asked.

'What could we tell them? You canny kid the cops. We told them everything.'

'Except where it is now,' Savage answered, grinning round at them all. ''Cause yous don't know. I know.'

'Well, we spent it, didn't we?' Skinny asked, looking at him dubiously.

'We spent nothing,' Savage derided him by his tone. 'I told you I had it stashed. What did we spend? A couple of hundred? Five hundred? What do you think?'

'I've no idea,' Skinny admitted.

'We spent nothing, nothing to what's left, nothing to what I took away,' Savage shouted at him, almost angrily.

He waved them to gather round and led them into the derelict air-raid shelter on the margin of the waste land, impatient to show them what he had hidden and to assert himself as their true boss because of the power he still had, the money he still had. The Brotherhood clustered in the cool dimness inside four brick walls, the floor only tramped earth, and listened to him offer them all the money they wanted. He was greater than Percy, he was smarter. He knew the cellar wouldn't be safe for long, he had been shifting the money for weeks and weeks, he had more than they had spent, ten times more than Percy took.

'There's loads and loads of it left,' he told them. 'I'm willing to share and share alike, and we can keep it for years and nobody'll ever be able to pin a damn thing on us. Yous willing? I'm willing!'

They wouldn't give in to him. They listened, but said

nothing. They were frightened. They wanted no part of it any longer. He knew they were right. They were only behaving as he expected.

'Okay then!' he cried viciously. 'Nobody else'll get it.'

He dragged out a chisel from the back pocket of his jeans and prised away four bricks from the wall near the tramped earth. When he straightened he had a bundle of fivers in his hand and he tore off the band, scattered the notes loose on the floor and then kicked them together with his foot, collecting them into a little pyramid. Specky, Skinny and Noddy, Cutchy, Pinky and Cuddy, and all the rag tag and bobtail of the Brotherhood watched him silently, suspiciously.

'Anybody want them?' he challenged.

Nobody moved, nobody spoke.

'Okay then,' he said once more, wagging a finger. 'Yous don't want it, I don't want it. Okay then, nobody else'll get it.'

He brought out the stump of a candle from his pocket, showed it round on the palm of his hand, and when they had all seen it he lit the wick with a loose match. The Brotherhood watched him sullenly, suspiciously. They didn't believe he would do it. He waved the lighted candle round and above his head till the flame seemed to form a continuous circle over him like a halo and grinned at the grim eyes staring at him.

'Burn it then!' he cried in an ecstasy of destructiveness and tossed the candle on to the little heap of notes.

A long-drawn gasp, like the involuntary sob of a sick man in mortal pain came from the circle of spectators and Savage laughed at them, a wild screech of joy.

The notes caught fire slowly, but when they burst into flame the wax of the candle melted in the heat and yellow tongues leapt high from the floor. The Brotherhood drew back a little. Those flames looked dangerous. But Savage was still cool. He went back to his cache and fetched out bundle after bundle after bundle of fivers till they thought he would never be done, all the money he had shifted secretly from the cellar since the day he had his own key made. He fed the flames carefully for a while with loose notes, a few at a time to keep the fire burning brightly, but he got impatient, he had so much to burn. He began to throw on whole bundles, without even taking the band off, and there was more smoke than flame.

Fits of coughing spread like an infection and Savage kindly raked the smouldering heap with the toe of his shoe to encourage the flames to leap out again. He chuckled happily as he tossed a last fistful on to the new blaze.

'That's the lot,' he turned and addressed the Brotherhood. 'Any complaints?'

They said nothing, but the dourness in the faces softened, dull eyes became brighter. They sagged in relief from doubt and anxiety, they breathed freely again like a patient who finds his illness wasn't mortal after all. Savage knew he had won. He was their master. He was the unchallenged leader of the pack, he could do what he liked with them. He threw his arms up, leapt like a ballet dancer high in the air, clicking his heels, and screamed to the roof.

'Yip-ee! Yip-ee! Yip-ee!'

He was inspired by the greatness of his action and went capering round the fire, whooping Red Indian war cries, his palm bobbing against his open lips, then down on his hunkers doing a Cossack dance. The frozen Brotherhood thawed completely in the warmth of his enthusiasm. Murmurs rustled through them like a wind in high corn and their feet itched to dance with their leader and their throats ached to howl with him.

Making a mockery of Percy's short-lived deity Savage began to chant the immemorial counting-out rhyme of Glasgow's back courts.

> 'El, el, domin-el,
> Eenty-teenty, figgerty-fel,
> You – are – OUT!'

He pounced on Specky, and Specky opened his mouth wide and let out the most blood-curdling screech ever heard in any shelter. He circled round the flaming money in his own version of a Comanche dance and drunk with Savage's insolence he too chanted.

> 'Eenty-teenty, figgerty-fel,
> Percy's in a prison cell,
> I saw the cops and widny tell,
> You – are – OUT!'

He tigged Skinny in his planetary course round the sun, and Skinny joined the dance, contributing squeakily.

> 'El, el, domin-el,
> Robin Hood and William Tell,
> Lawman, gunman, shot and shell,
> You – are – OUT!'

He claimed Noddy in transit, but Noddy scorned to add to the chant. The only music he loved was what he could wheedle from a mouth-organ, what he hoped to coax from a piano one day if he succeeded in keeping the money he had hidden in the lavatory cistern. Still, to prove he had the true party spirit, he did a cartwheel, walked on his hands for twenty paces, and tumbled his wulcats. The rest of the Brotherhood surged exultantly forward and soon they were all in the fire-dance, whooping and hopping in a circle, right hand on the right shoulder of the comrade in front as they all swayed to the rhythm of *El-el, domin-el*.

Savage broke off at a tangent and ran to a corner where he kicked away a pile of causies, bent down lithely and came up with the big brass bell, the old school bell Percy had forbidden him to hawk. It was his now. Returning to the blaze he sergeant-majored the dancers, bawling out to inject the flagging chant with new strength.

> 'El, el, domin-el,
> We've lit the candle, now ring the bell!
> Garson shopped to save himsel',
> Let the bastard rot in hell,
> He – ran – OUT!'

He rang the bell three times, and the Brotherhood halted and bowed their heads in mock reverence at that reminder of Percy's ritual.

'Yip-ee!' screamed Savage and whipped them on again. They picked up the steps, roaring together rhythmically, 'Yah! Yay! Yah-yah-yah!' Savage herded them as an outrider, ringing the bell at every third step.

He rang it too often. And the ringing of the bell led to the end of their burial service for the god El and in a few moments they were scattered like leaves before the wild west wind for the stranger in the belted raincoat was crossing the wasteland just as their dance round the burning money was at its noisiest. He too was fully informed by Press and radio of all that had happened, but when he learned that Percy had been lifted with about three thousand pounds on him he was far from satisfied the game was over. There was too much more still to be accounted for, too much for a gang of schoolboys to have spent in three months. He swore, and swore to find where the rest of it was.

In the afternoon he had asked at the hospital for Savage, pretending to be an uncle worried about the condition of his nephew. When he was told Savage had left in the morning to go to speak to the police it was just something more he didn't believe. Savage and not Percy now seemed to have the key to the mystery. By tea-time he was prowling round Bethel Street, Ossian Street and Tulip Place, hopefully looking for school-boys. The trouble was he didn't know what Savage looked like. But he couldn't just go away and do nothing. He had to keep looking for schoolboys, because until he found them he wouldn't find Savage. One of them might say something, one of them might lead him somewhere. But there were no school-boys to be seen. He had never known the area so empty of boys. He stopped hanging about the back-streets and went through the closes in Bethel Street desperate for some boys he could quiz. There was no point hanging about near the cellar. Nobody would go into the cellar now. Anyway it wasn't likely the money was still there. If Percy had run away with so little, some-body else must have already shifted more. And that some-body else was Savage. He was sure of his deduction, proud of his shrewdness, but it didn't bring Savage any nearer.

He went into the back court, but there were no boys there either. He went sideways through a bent railing into the waste ground and blundered over towards the Steamie, and that was when he heard the bell ringing in the air-raid shelter. He stopped, looked and listened. He saw a thin trail of smoke coming out of the entrance, he heard the hub-bub of boyish trebles, and then the bell again, and again. He moved over stealthily, peered in cautiously, saw the blazing paper on the floor, the boys dancing round it, an acrobat doing somersaults, a midget all topsy-turvy walking on his hands, whirling dervishes, howling wolves and laughing hyenas. But boys for all that. That was all he wanted. Boys. He had come to the end of the line. He knew it. He dashed in like a commando attacking an enemy outpost single-handed.

Then he saw it was indeed the end of the line. He saw the flames leaping from the bright apex of the pyramid and on the slopes, curled with the heat, already licked by eager tongues, he saw the fivers and recognized the imprint of the bank. They seemed to be drawing the flames to themselves like a magnet, and nothing could save them.

As quickly as the stranger recognized the banknotes Savage recognized the stranger Percy had warned them about. He held the bell by the clapper, raised his free hand to hush his brothers, and stepped forward boldly to con-front the intruder, a savage chief despising the white man come in quest of native wealth.

'You're too late, Mac,' he announced insolently. 'That's the lot there. We couldn't use it, you're not going to get it.'

He saw no need to mention the fifty fivers he had inside his leather jacket.

The stranger gawked, his throat working as if he was going to be sick on the spot.

'You stupid bastard!' he moaned, and dived at the fire trying to save something, burned his fingers, and yelped.

Savage laughed. The Brotherhood laughed.

The stranger knelt by the victorious fire and whined up at them.

'Yous didn't know what you were doing. Yous were too young to get a chance like that. You hadn't the brains to make use of it. There was enough there to set a man up for life. You could have had heaven on earth wi' what was there, and you've burned it, you've burned it. You set all that money on fire! Oh, Christ, yous are mad!'

The Brotherhood gathered round, looking down on him, and then their unconcerned laughter changed to a silent awe when they saw tears rolling down the stranger's cheeks. They looked away, too embarrassed to watch a grown man weeping like a wean and wringing his hands. The stranger jumped to his feet and went berserk. He dived in amongst them, hitting out viciously, and they yielded ground, retreating to the exit. Then on a common impulse they made an about turn and scattered, leaving him to rake amongst the ashes for at least one whole fiver out of thirty thousand pounds. He didn't find one.

And while he crouched alone in the air-raid shelter sobbing and cursing, O'Neill and O'Donnell were having a cool pint in the Tappit Hen.

'Did you see what was in last night's paper?' said O'Neill. 'It's jist what I was telling you a couple of months back.'

'Ach, they get swelt-heidit, some of the young yins,' said O'Donnell. 'They play a couple of seasons and then they think they're worth a lot of money so they ask for a transfer. But he's no' the first that's had a quarrel wi' the Celtic and the club aye gets on without them.'

'No' him,' said O'Neill. 'The weans that found the money I mean. Though mind you I was wan o' the first to say he was getting in bad with the club. I seen it coming.'

'Oh aye, I seen it,' said O'Donnell. 'Imagine a lad of seventeen finding it and dishing it out to a crowd o' weans. Of course he had a grievance. They dropped him for the semi-final remember. But you notice they're no' saying where it came from.'

'Maybe they don't know,' said O'Neill. 'That would be a laugh, eh? And I telt ye, that's only wan o' them. There's mair to come yet. You see, it was a matter of discipline, he broke the training. He's no' the first star Celtic have dropped before a big game, and anyway they went on and won the Cup without him. A boy of seventeen is all he was, kind of glaikit from what I heard. My good-sister knows his mother. She used to live up the same close.'

'His mother's an Orangewoman, she was heartbroken when he signed for the green and white,' said O'Donnell.

'No' his mother, the Phinn wan's mother,' said O'Neill.

'Ah but he was clever, you've got to admit it,' said O'Donnell. 'I've saw him travel the whole length of the park and so help me God you'd think the ball was tied to his laces. He was a real artist, ye canny deny it.'

'It's like these modern weapons,' said O'Neill. 'Power in the hands o' folks that's no' fit to use it.'

'He used it all right against the Rangers the last Ne'erday game,' said O'Donnell. 'But isn't it damnable the now? All ye get in the papers on a Saturday night is golf and tennis and cricket. Who the hell's interested?'

'No' him, the weans,' said O'Neill. 'All that money. They could never spend that amount o' money. That's what I'm trying to tell ye. Power in the hauns o' folk that's no' fit for it. If it had been you or me it would have been different. We could have retired. D'ye know the money spent on armaments every year would let a man no' need to work mair than two days a week?'

'I still say the Celtic could do wi' mair like him,' said O'Donnell impatiently. 'And anyway tell me, what would you do if you hadn't your work to go to?'

'I suppose you're right,' said O'Neill.

A SELECTION OF POPULAR READING IN PAN

NON-FICTION

Translated and edited by Ian Scott based on the original
German text by Dr Max Lüscher
THE LÜSCHER COLOUR TEST   50p
Harrison E. Salisbury
THE 900 DAYS: The Siege Of Leningrad   95p
David Reuben, M.D.
EVERYTHING YOU ALWAYS WANTED TO
  KNOW ABOUT SEX but were afraid to ask   45p
Peter F. Drucker
THE AGE OF DISCONTINUITY   60p
Norman Mailer
A FIRE ON THE MOON   40p
Leonard Mosley
ON BORROWED TIME (illus)   65p
Margaret Powell
CLIMBING THE STAIRS   25p
Adrian Hill
HOW TO DRAW (illus)   30p
edited by Bruce Campbell
THE COUNTRYMAN WILD LIFE BOOK (illus)   30p
Andrew Duncan
THE REALITY OF MONARCHY   40p
Graham Hill
LIFE AT THE LIMIT (illus)   35p
Ken Welsh
HITCH-HIKER'S GUIDE TO EUROPE   35p
Miss Read
MISS READ'S COUNTRY COOKING   30p
Gavin Maxwell
RAVEN SEEK THY BROTHER (illus)   30p

Obtainable from all booksellers and newsagents. If you have
any difficulty, please send purchase price plus 5p postage to
P.O. Box 11, Falmouth, Cornwall. While every effort is
made to keep prices low, it is sometimes necessary to increase
prices at short notice. PAN Books reserve the right to show
new retail prices on covers which may differ from the text
or elsewhere.